"I should've done this earlier," Lucas whispered into her wild and unruly hair. His protective arms wound around her, tucking her in tight.

"It's nice to see you, Gwen. You look stunning as always, and I'm glad you're here." He released her too soon, gripping her shoulders gently and fixing her with a determined gaze. "I don't know what's going on back in New Plymouth, but I meant what I said about protecting you any way I can. A lot of things have changed between us, but not that. Never that."

"It looks like your bill has been paid," the cashier said brightly.

"What?" Lucas asked. "By who?"

The uneasy sensation of being watched rode over Gwen's skin once more, and she clutched on to Lucas's sleeve for support.

"Are you sure you've got the right table?" Lucas asked, a clear measure of disbelief in his tone. "We were alone in the corner booth."

"Positive," the cashier said pertly. "There's even a note in the register's memo. Must've been a friend. It says 'Welcome home.'"

SVU Surveillance deals with topics some readers might find difficult, such as sexual assault and the PTSD that follows as a result.

SVU
SURVEILLANCE

—

Julie Anne Lindsey

HARLEQUIN
INTRIGUE

For Alicia Wright.

HARLEQUIN®
I N T R I G U E®

Recycling programs
for this product may
not exist in your area.

ISBN-13: 978-1-335-40160-1

SVU Surveillance

Copyright © 2021 by Julie Anne Lindsey

All rights reserved. No part of this book may be used or reproduced in
any manner whatsoever without written permission except in the case of
brief quotations embodied in critical articles and reviews.

This is a work of fiction. Names, characters, places and incidents
are either the product of the author's imagination or are used fictitiously.
Any resemblance to actual persons, living or dead, businesses,
companies, events or locales is entirely coincidental.

This edition published by arrangement with Harlequin Books S.A.

For questions and comments about the quality of this book,
please contact us at CustomerService@Harlequin.com.

Harlequin Enterprises ULC
22 Adelaide St. West, 40th Floor
Toronto, Ontario M5H 4E3, Canada
www.Harlequin.com

Printed in U.S.A.

Julie Anne Lindsey is an obsessive reader who was once torn between the love of her two favorite genres: toe-curling romance and chew-your-nails suspense. Now she gets to write both for Harlequin Intrigue. When she's not creating new worlds, Julie can be found carpooling her three kids around northeastern Ohio and plotting with her shamelessly enabling friends. Winner of the Daphne du Maurier Award for Excellence in Mystery/Suspense, Julie is a member of International Thriller Writers, Romance Writers of America and Sisters in Crime. Learn more about Julie and her books at julieannelindsey.com.

Books by Julie Anne Lindsey

Harlequin Intrigue

Heartland Heroes

SVU Surveillance

Fortress Defense

Deadly Cover-Up
Missing in the Mountains
Marine Protector
Dangerous Knowledge

Garrett Valor

Shadow Point Deputy
Marked by the Marshal

Protectors of Cade County

Federal Agent Under Fire
The Sheriff's Secret

Visit the Author Profile page at Harlequin.com.

CAST OF CHARACTERS

Gwen Kind—The victim of a near-deadly attack during homecoming week her senior year of college. Gwen spent the last six years building a safe but lonely life for herself one town away. Until someone leaves a flyer on her windshield, inviting her back for homecoming week, and she's suddenly unsure she was ever really safe at all.

Lucas Winchester—Gwen's former fiancé and current West Liberty SVU detective. Lucas gave up a future in architecture to seek revenge on Gwen's attacker. Despite the fact he hasn't spoken to Gwen in six years, the only thing he wants more than her love is justice for what she's been through. Thanks to a recent turn of events, he might finally get both.

Derek Winchester—Oldest of the Winchester siblings. A PI with an attitude. A rebel and a wild card. Always ready to help his brothers.

Isaac Winchester—Youngest of the four Winchesters. A cousin by blood, brother by upbringing and paramedic by trade. Determined to save the world, one patient at a time.

Blaze Winchester—West Liberty homicide detective, and Lucas Winchester's older brother, assisting in the search for Gwen's abductor.

Detective Andrews—New Plymouth SVU detective assigned to Gwen's case.

Phillip Cranston—Undergraduate professor from Gwen's college days.

Chapter One

Gwen Kind bent to stretch her hamstrings and catch her breath beside the busiest jogging path in New Plymouth, Kentucky. She'd hoped to shake the icky sensation of being watched off her sweaty skin before heading home, but that clearly wasn't going to happen.

She stood and twisted at the waist, pulling in deep lungfuls of crisp autumn air, then watching the little puffs of breath float away in frosty clouds. October was beautiful in New Plymouth, distractingly so. With the trees showing off their fanciest colors, the city planting endless bunches of gold, crimson and purple mums, and shop owners lining sidewalks in pumpkin-topped hay bales, what wasn't to love? Gwen particularly liked the fact that every downtown window seemed to advertise something flavored or scented in apple cinnamon and mulling spice.

In the park, folks had donned their cool-weather best. Zipped and tucked into brightly colored jackets and hats, they were a hundred dots of human confetti moving across the still green grass. A worn rubber trail ebbed and flowed through clusters of meticulously landscaped trees and around a lake continually packed with geese. Metro Park was never empty, so this was where Gwen would jog now. Even if that meant dodging moms with double strollers and dogs on long leashes, or being occasionally knocked into by folks on bikes, skateboards or Rollerblades.

She preferred her morning runs along the county's less-traveled hike-and-bike trail before work, but lately the solitary path had left her feeling uneasy and distinctly paranoid. She'd nearly sprinted back to her car on the last trip there, certain she wasn't alone, but unable to see anything besides a handful of squirrels and the occasional flock of birds among the trees. Still, instinct insisted she change her routine, and experience agreed. After all, it had only been six years since Gwen had been brutally attacked during her college's homecoming weekend. Raped, beaten and cut. Then left unconscious after a night out with friends.

She fished her car key from her pocket with a sigh. She missed the hike-and-bike trail, but she'd survive. She'd given up many more important things in the name of safety. Losing her favorite place to run was hardly a sacrifice in comparison. Even if Metro Park was a congested nightmare. She gave the area another visual sweep before making the final trek back to the large public parking area beside the busy downtown street.

She checked under the car on her approach, looked nearby men in their eyes, then peered into the back seat before unlocking and opening her door. She dropped immediately behind the wheel and locked up once more, then settled herself for the ride home. At least traffic wouldn't be bad with half the population already at the park.

The drive home was quick and easy, the day bright and pleasant with an unseasonably cold chill. The weatherman had thrown the word *snow* around this morning, making her wonder yet again why she'd relocated to New Plymouth, only one town away from her former college, when she could've stayed with her family in Florida. She'd told her parents she feared her attacker would expect her to go home, and starting over somewhere completely new made her feel safer. It wasn't a lie, but in hindsight she suspected her real motivation for staying in the area had more to do with being a stone's throw from her former fiancé than anything else. Silly, but knowing he was across the county instead of across the country had been a great comfort during the worst of times.

Gwen turned onto her street, then motored into her one-car attached garage and closed the door behind her before getting out. She unlocked the door to her home, then locked it behind her and pressed her code into the keypad beside the coatrack, silencing the alarm system.

She'd chosen the one-story open-floor-plan home for its small, manageable footprint and proximity to town. Just over a thousand square feet with postage-stamp front and back yards. The furnishings were minimal, but brightly colored and purchased locally to avoid the stark utilitarian look her mother continually complained about during her visits. Gwen liked that the place was easy to monitor and protect.

Forty minutes and a quick shower later, she was back

in the car, hair clean but damp and wound into her usual tidy bun. She'd traded the running gear and shoes for a gray pantsuit and flats, then performed a speedy lip balm and mascara makeup routine.

The sensation of being watched struck again as her car hit the street beyond her driveway. She checked her mirrors, examining the empty lawns and silent homes around her before shifting into Drive and rolling slowly away. The paranoia grew as she traveled, despite her best efforts to will it away. She practiced controlled breathing and reminded herself that these feelings were normal for someone who'd been through what she had. That PTSD could linger for decades. And she was safe.

Gwen sighed in relief as her office came into view, then waved at a familiar pair of women on the sidewalk. She hurried to park and catch up with them before they reached the front doors. "Good morning," she called, forcing a smile as she ran.

The women stopped outside a towering set of glass doors.

The historic brick building behind them had once been five stories of run-down apartments, but a recent conversion by her bosses had changed all that. Noble Architecture and Design had gutted the interior and created a phoenix from the rubble. Now the building's face was predominantly glass, and the inside was two soaring floors of design studios with spectacular downtown views.

"You look flushed," Marina, the older of the two women, said as Gwen hustled to reach them. She fastened another button on her white wool coat while she waited. "Or are you glowing? Is there a man?" She drew out the final word in a dramatic singsong way, as was her custom, and Gwen instinctively slowed her pace. The curvy mother of four never tired of trying to find Gwen a date, but Gwen had long ago tired of hearing about it.

"No man," Gwen answered, a hint of aggravation in her tone. She shook her head and smiled to soften the response. It wasn't Marina's fault she didn't understand Gwen's reluctance to date, or know the reasoning behind the decision. No one in New Plymouth did. "I've been running at Metro Park," she added in explanation of her flushed skin. "It was packed before work, so I'm a little behind schedule."

Marina's assistant, Debbie, gave Gwen a once-over. Her heavily lined eyes narrowed and her ruby lips pulled to one side. "I thought you jogged the hike-and-bike trail before work?"

"I do, but the Metro Park gets so much buzz, I thought I'd see what all the fuss was about," Gwen improvised.

"So?" Marina asked, her warm olive skin aglow. "How was it?"

"A definite hotspot from six thirty to seven fifteen a.m.," Gwen groused.

Marina grinned. "I'll bet that makes it a great place to meet people. Young, single people." She worked her eyebrows up and down.

Gwen laughed. "Enough about me. I'm waiting to hear how dinner went last night. Did the kids like the new casserole?" she asked, redirecting the conversation as she held the door for the other women.

Marina let her head drop forward as she crossed the threshold. "Don't get me started." She lifted her stricken face, then dove into a detailed play-by-play on her family's meal preferences and quirks. Debbie hung on every word, and Gwen was officially off the hook for discussion.

The ladies parted ways inside the design studios, and Gwen got lost in her administrative work. The day was a blur of invoicing and phone calls, testing Gwen's concentration and time management skills to the max. Then, just as quickly as it had begun, another day was over.

Her coworkers donned their coats and hats, then moved in a wave toward the elevator doors.

Gwen hustled to keep up. "Hold the elevator!" she called, pressing herself into the already-packed car. She didn't make a habit of being alone anywhere other than her home, and she had a bottle of wine waiting for her there. Plus a half slice of chocolate cake she couldn't wait to finish off.

The car's passengers shifted to make room as she pinned her body between Marina and a tall man in Armani. "Hey, Collin," she said, hoping to sound casual in the awkward position.

"Gwen," he said with a smile. "I stopped by to say hello earlier, but you seemed busy. I didn't want to bother you."

She pressed her lips together and nodded, trying not to think about his body pressed tightly to hers.

The doors parted a moment later, and the passengers spilled into the first-floor foyer.

Collin kept an easy pace at Gwen's side. They made their way back through the glass doors and into the chilly evening. She rolled her shoulders and breathed easier with the added space between them. "Already dark," she muttered, hating autumn for the singular inconvenience and heading for her car at a clip.

Marina and the other designers spoke in hushed tones a few feet behind, likely talking about Collin and his noteworthy physique.

"I think they're talking about me," Collin said with a grin.

"This is my car," Gwen announced, unwilling to bite. Her unremarkable sedan was bathed in a cone of lamplight. She couldn't see beneath the vehicle without bending down, but trusted her coworkers wouldn't let anyone drag her away without a fight.

Collin smiled.

"You already know that," she said. Just like she knew he drove the sleek black sports car parked a few rows away. "Sorry."

He shrugged. "Got any plans for the weekend?"

Netflix and chill crossed her mind, except in Gwen's world the phrase was extremely literal and done alone. "Maybe. You?"

"I'm thinking about dinner at La Maison Blanche. Any chance I can convince you to join me?"

She smiled, but shook her head. "I can't. I—"

"Say no more." He raised a hand and returned her

smile. "Can't blame a guy for trying. Another night, then?"

"Maybe."

His expression brightened as he turned to walk backward, moving in the direction of his car. "That's not a no," he said. "And I'm nothing if not dedicated to a good cause. See you tomorrow, Kind."

She lifted one hand in a hip-high wave, then waited before turning around.

Marina and the other designers were blatantly eavesdropping from their nearby cars.

The older women waved innocently as Collin drove away.

Victoria Noble, owner of the design group, was the first to speak. "Are you crazy?" she asked. "Collin is smitten with you, and he's perfect. Have you seen his backside?"

Gwen snorted, suddenly absolutely certain of what the others had been whispering about behind them. Her humor faded, however, as the icy fingers of unease slid down her spine. The too-familiar sensation of being watched settled hot on her cheeks.

"She's blushing," Marina called. "We've embarrassed her. We're sorry, sweetie. We're just suckers for love."

"And that heinie," Victoria added.

Gwen's chest constricted, and the world began to tilt. She turned in search of an onlooker, but saw no one.

"We'll see you tomorrow, hon," Marina called.

Gwen raised a palm absently before dropping into her car and locking the doors.

A folded sheet of paper came immediately into view, flapping gently against her windshield where it was trapped beneath one wiper blade. For a moment, she debated leaving it there, driving away without accepting it, whatever it was. She didn't need another take-out menu. Didn't want to see a local band or run a 5K for charity. And she didn't want to get back out of her locked car, alone at night in the parking lot.

She stared at the offending flyer. If she left it stuck there, it would probably blow off in traffic, and Gwen wasn't a litterbug. She steeled her nerves, then jumped out to snatch the paper and return to her position behind the wheel. She tossed the page onto the passenger seat and locked the doors.

The dashboard vents piped hot air throughout the small space and rustled the paper, drawing her attention to the sheet once more.

A familiar logo registered with each flap of the folded sheet. She reached carefully across the car, as if the flyer might attack, then pressed the paper open. Air rushed from her lungs as she took the message in.

It wasn't a take-out menu, marketing for a band or a local 5K.

It was an invitation to the Bellemont College Homecoming.

Chapter Two

Lucas Winchester slammed the receiver of his desktop phone in frustration. Some days, being a West Liberty Special Victims Unit Detective was exactly what he'd signed up for. Most days it wasn't, and today was one of those. He scrubbed angry hands against his stubble-covered cheeks and swore. He'd hauled low-level street thug and repeat-rapist Tommy Black in three times in two years, and he'd hoped yesterday's arrest would be the last. Somehow the scumbag got off every time. A loophole or technicality. And unlike Lucas, Tommy was having a stellar day. According to the Bond Enforcement officer who'd dialed Lucas as a courtesy, someone had posted Tommy's bail. Now the creep was on the loose again. Bad news for his favorite victim, an on-again, off-again girlfriend he frequently beat, and also raped, from time to time.

Lucas stared at the silent phone. He had to tell Anise that her abuser was out again.

He should've been an architect. Should've listened to his folks and his professors, but the little voice in his head was too loud to be ignored. *Be a cop. Make a dif-*

ference. Be someone's hero. That was what he'd told himself before he knew how frequently the system let people down. When he'd been a peripheral victim of injustice, he'd blamed the terrible officers who'd obviously missed something and completely dropped the ball. These days he knew better. Lucas was a damn good cop, and criminals walked every day. One way or another.

He stretched his neck and gave himself a mental kick in the pants. Then he dialed Anise and gave her the news. The conversation went as poorly as expected. He encouraged her to make a statement, press charges and testify in court, but she refused. Rightfully afraid of Tommy, and certain Lucas would fail her again. He couldn't blame her for that. How could he? Anise swore vehemently at him before hanging up.

"Today sucks," he muttered, shaking a pair of aspirin into his palm. He kept a bottle the size of a football in his drawer, right beside a matching tub of antacids. *Thank you, Big Box Store.* He washed the pair of pills down with the dregs of his stone-cold coffee, thankful it was finally quitting time.

Based on the rumble of footfalls and familiar voices outside his office, Lucas wasn't the only one whose shift was over. His coworkers would get a drink together and blow off some steam before heading home to their families. Lucas had wild plans for uninterrupted solitude and maybe another self-loathing pass at the piles of worn-and-tattered files in his guest-room-turned-office. The five-year-old cold case had started him on his current path, though the case hadn't been cold at the time.

Nowadays, Lucas was the terrible officer who couldn't name or apprehend the violent rapist.

"Winchester!" Bruce, a detective twenty years his senior, called before swinging through the open door with a small entourage at his back. "Beers and burgers. Let's go!"

Lucas kicked his open desk drawer shut and forced a tight smile. "Not tonight." He stretched onto his feet and threaded his arms into the worn leather jacket he'd had since college.

"Another hot date?" Bruce asked, sounding a little too impressed by the possibility.

Lucas tugged a knit cap over his shaggy hair and grinned. "Hey, don't worry, Bruce. Your wife always turns me down."

The group laughed.

Bruce scoffed. "Yeah, right. I don't believe that for a minute. Look at you, all *GQ*. I'm still wearing the loafers I wore when you were sworn in."

Lucas shouldered his bag and pocketed his keys, then led the way toward the exit.

"Who's the woman?" Bruce pressed, sticking close to his heels.

"You don't know her."

Bruce made a throaty noise behind him. "Of course I don't know her. I'm married thirty years. I got three kids in Catholic school. Who do I know besides them and the priest?"

"Then why ask?" Lucas challenged.

Bruce edged in beside him, shoulders raised to his ears. "I want to know more people. Where do you meet all these women? They aren't students at the college are they?"

Lucas groaned inwardly, certain the hallway was getting longer with each step. It was his fault really. He'd paraded a string of pointless dates through the local pub several years back and made a name for himself as a playboy among cops, which was saying something. It had been a failed attempt to move on with his new life, using women and booze as a distraction. Then, he'd made his first big arrest and everything changed. Suddenly the only distraction he needed was the thrill of the chase and the victory of seeing violent offenders get what they deserved. He'd cleaned himself up, stopped trying to replace the one woman who meant everything with a dozen who meant nothing and took up jogging to clear his head. Thankfully, his bad reputation still got him out of drinks with the boys whenever he wanted.

"Really," Bruce pushed. "Who is she this time?"

She, Lucas thought, was the smart, sassy, fun-loving woman he'd met on campus his junior year at Bellemont College. The same woman who'd promptly and irrevocably stolen his heart. Then broken it.

"You never bring your ladies out anymore," Bruce said. "Some of us are married, but we're not dead. We liked seeing your flavors of the month."

"Month?" Another detective laughed. "You mean week?"

Lucas glanced over his shoulder and shook his head. It was too easy to keep up the facade. These guys did all the work on their own.

A woman cleared her throat in front of them, and

Lucas spun back. The group halted sharply, rocking collectively on their heels. "Pardon me, detectives," Officer Kim Lake said, looking wholly unimpressed by the conversation she'd clearly overheard. "Detective Winchester is needed in the conference room." She hooked a thumb over one shoulder, indicating the open door several feet away.

The group clapped him on the back as they strode past, probably thankful not to be the one held up at quitting time.

Lucas did his best not to seem disappointed. "What is it, Kim?"

"There's a woman asking to see you."

Lucas frowned back at her. "Someone's here to file a report?" He didn't normally take the reports. Cases were assigned to him.

"No, she's asking for you. By name." Kim crossed her arms. "And I don't think she's here on a personal visit. She looks too smart to put up with any of your nonsense."

Lucas grinned. "Fair," he said. "Reporter?"

"Didn't say." Kim turned to stand beside him, staring in the direction of the open conference room door. "She seems shaken, so I wouldn't peg her for a reporter, but she wouldn't say more. Only that she needs to talk with you, Luke Winchester."

"Luke?" he asked, moving around Kim toward the open door.

"Yeah."

No one had called Lucas that in years. No one at the precinct ever had.

Instinct clawed at the back of his neck as he lengthened his strides. "Thanks."

He knocked on the door frame with a spear of anticipation, determined to look both professional and approachable. "Sorry to keep you waiting. I'm Detective—" The words clogged in his throat. His limbs froze, and his heart rate spiked at the sight of the barely recognizable woman before him.

But even six years later, her wild red curls tamed into a bun and wearing a high-end pantsuit instead of cutoffs and his old concert shirts, Lucas knew her instantly.

"Gwen."

Chapter Three

Lucas led Gwen into O'Grady's Pub, a place they'd frequented together in another lifetime, and one he'd avoided every day since. Still, O'Grady's had seemed like the best alternative when Gwen insisted on speaking privately, but not at the precinct. She hadn't said much more than that, and her silence had Lucas's nerves on edge. As if it wasn't enough that she'd shown up out of the blue like this, now she had a secret, too.

He scanned the multitude of faces as they threaded their way through the tightly packed space. Music thumped from overhead speakers and voices rose in waves, cheering at televised ball games and real-life rounds of darts. The beloved pub was only a few blocks from campus and downtown, making it a hotspot for civilians and especially unpopular with the cops who took too much interest in Lucas's personal life. For that reason alone, the place was perfect.

"Wow," Gwen muttered, taking in the static decor and general commotion. "This place hasn't changed."

"Not at all," he agreed. "The nostalgia is strong here." Thankfully, so were the drinks.

His thoughts, however, were erratic, confused and demanding. What had brought Gwen back to West Liberty after all this time? Why hadn't she told him yet? And why not just call?

Probably because she never called, he thought dryly. *Not in six years.*

She stopped at a small corner booth away from the crowd. "This okay?"

He dipped his chin, slightly aggravated by the secrecy and mild theatrics that had never been Gwen's way.

She dropped her purse on the heavily lacquered table, then slid onto the cracked red vinyl seat, facing the door and window.

Reluctantly, Lucas settled on the bench across from her with his back to the door. He clasped his hands on the tabletop and waited. Patience was a skill preached endlessly at the academy, one he wasn't any good at. "Ready to tell me what this is about yet?"

Her wide brown eyes snapped to his, and she matched his posture, twining her fingers on the table. "I'm sorry I didn't call first."

He shrugged. "It's no problem." He couldn't get a bead on her mood. Nervous, obviously, but why? Being back in this town? Being there with him? She'd marched into the precinct wanting to see him for something. It'd be great if she got around to explaining what that was. He clenched his jaw against the possibility she'd come to announce she was getting married and didn't want him to hear it from anyone else first.

"Do you need to call anyone?" she asked, projecting her voice against the din of rowdy patrons.

The question caught him off guard and drew him back to the moment, confused again. "Who?"

Gwen frowned. "From where I was sitting earlier, it sounded as if you might have a hot date."

Lucas fought the urge to laugh, opting instead to remove his jacket and toss it onto the bench beside him. Heat coursed up his neck at the memory of Bruce and the others teasing him in the hallway. "I don't need to call anyone."

She rolled her eyes. "How are your folks?"

"Good. Yours?"

"Fine."

"Gwen," he whispered, leaning across the table. "Whatever brought you here. Whatever you want to say. Just say it. I can't react until I know what this is about."

She shifted, pulling her hands into her lap. A flash of uncertainty crossed her pretty face, and she chewed her bottom lip. "Someone invited me to homecoming."

"Homecoming?" Lucas let the words circle, then settle, in his heart and head. After what had happened to her at homecoming six years back, it seemed a strange and senseless statement. Who would do that? And why had she made the trip to town to tell Lucas? "Do I know him?" he asked, hoping it wasn't one of his idiot college roommates. Should he care if it was? Did she want him to care?

"I don't know," she said softly, dragging the silver zipper open on her purse. She reached inside and removed a folded sheet of paper with trembling fingers.

"It could be nothing," she said, her expression both apologetic and hopeful. "If it's nothing, then I don't want to talk about it, and I'll be on my way. But if it's something, I knew I couldn't talk to anyone other than you."

"Let me see." Lucas took the paper and fanned it open with unnecessary force, then smoothed it on the table between them. "Join Bellemont College staff and students for a week of homecoming fun," he read. He'd seen variations of the same flyer posted all over town, printed in the newspaper and splashed generously across local media all month. "I don't get it." He raised his eyes to hers once more, trying and failing to understand the reason one folded flyer had drawn her out of hiding and delivered her to his door.

A tear slid over the curve of her pink cheek, and she swiped it away with one shaky hand. "I know."

Her whisper gonged in the too-loud, overcrowded bar, pounding straight through Lucas's heart. He released the flyer to scrub a palm across his mouth. "Sorry." Coming back to West Liberty wasn't easy for her. The least he could do was be patient while she got to her point. Assuming she had one. "Who invited you to homecoming?"

Another tear fell, erased by a quick, determined hand. "I don't know."

Lucas straightened, eyes narrowing. "What do you mean, you don't know? Where'd you get the flyer?"

"I found it tucked under my windshield wiper after work." Gwen swallowed and wet her lips. "No one else's car had one."

Tension wound through his limbs. A hundred heinous thoughts presented in his brain. "When you said you were invited to homecoming. This is what you meant?" Suddenly things made more sense. Her visit. Her mood. "You think it was a message?" He bit his tongue against the thing neither of them would say. *A message from her rapist.* A man who had never been caught.

Her eyes misted, and she pressed her pink lips tight.

"Hey, y'all!" a perky blonde called upon approach. Her O'Grady's T-shirt and apron over blue jeans announced her as pub staff. "What can I get y'all started with?"

Gwen worked up a smile. "White wine. And fries."

The waitress grinned. "Gotcha." She flicked her gaze to Lucas. "For you?"

"House ale on tap," he said, not caring what she brought. The beer was officially a prop to put Gwen at ease. Her visit wasn't personal. It was business, which meant Lucas was on duty. Hopefully the glass of wine Gwen ordered would help her relax enough to tell the rest of her story in detail. The more he knew, the better chance he had at helping.

"Anything else?" the waitress asked.

Lucas trailed his gaze over Gwen's narrow jaw and frame. "Chips and salsa. Burger sliders. For the table."

Gwen waited for the waitress to leave before returning her attention to him. The tears were gone and fresh resolution burned in her eyes. "I started feeling as if I was being watched about three weeks ago. I wasn't sure at first, because I still get paranoid like that sometimes. Usually, it's a moment here or there. Nothing that sticks.

Then a few weeks ago, the sensation never really left. Instead, it's gotten progressively worse, and today after work, there was a flyer for homecoming on my windshield. I understand it could be nothing, but I think it's time I get a second opinion."

Lucas ground his teeth at the possibility someone was following her, frightening her. "Any chance someone you know is messing with you?" he asked, trying to rule out the more likely and less dangerous possibilities first. "Maybe this person doesn't know the extent of what you've been through, only that you never visit your alma mater, and they wanted to tease you about it for some reason?"

"No." She kneaded her hands on the table. "I've never told anyone about what happened to me at Bellemont. No one even knows I went to college there. I didn't include the school on my résumé."

He frowned, wondering selfishly if she'd erased him from her revised history, as well. "What do you do for a living that didn't require your degree?" he asked, sticking to a safer subject. He didn't know a lot about fashion, but the suit, heels and handbag all seemed to scream corporate. And when he'd met her, she had been on track to be a very successful engineer.

"I'm an administrative assistant at the Noble Architecture and Design Firm in New Plymouth."

"New Plymouth." The town name nearly took him as off guard as her career choice. Gwen was living only one town away. "How long have you been back from Florida?"

Gwen lowered her eyes again, choosing to study her

manicure, then their surroundings. "I only stayed with my parents for a few months. I told myself I had to come back and get on with living." She shrugged out of her coat and folded it on the bench beside her, then set her purse on top. "I got a job, eventually bought a home. But I couldn't bring myself to go back to Belle-mont and finish those last few classes, so I didn't. What was one more change when my life was already topsy-turvy, right?"

"I suppose." Lucas took a moment to process the information and appreciate the subtle changes.

Gwen was beautiful as always, if thinner. Her formerly curvy figure was lean, almost willowy and her skin slightly sun-kissed despite the plummeting temperatures.

"You're still jogging."

She grimaced, as if he'd hit a sore spot. "It used to be the only time I felt completely unburdened, but that's different now, too."

The waitress returned with their drinks, and Gwen took a long sip of her wine. She traced a fingertip along the condensation of her glass, then told her story in full, filling Lucas in on the significant details of her last few weeks. How she felt unsafe at her usual jogging spot and hated the new one. How she felt watched outside her home and work. And worried she might be losing her mind.

"Have you considered getting a guard dog?" Lucas asked.

"I have," she said, "but I wouldn't want to leave him

home alone all day while I'm at work, and I wouldn't want to go out alone at night to walk him."

"How about a husband?" he asked, hoping to sound playful instead of jealous at the thought.

"No men," she said, her tone strangely sharp. "I don't date."

Lucas lifted his palms in apology, obviously hitting another nerve.

The waitress returned with their food and a second glass of wine for Gwen, then vanished into the crowd once more.

Lucas sipped his beer and processed all he'd learned. He pushed the chips and sliders into the table's center, indicating Gwen should help herself. His insides had tightened beyond the ability to eat the moment he'd realized she could be right. The son of a gun who'd left her for dead could be back and coming for her again. And what could Lucas do to stop him?

She snagged a fry and forced a tight smile. "Well, what do you think, Detective Winchester? Do I have reason to worry? Or am I being paranoid?"

Lucas flicked his attention to the flyer before leveling her with his most protective stare. "I don't like it," he said honestly. "And I don't believe in coincidences. But you can be sure I won't let anyone hurt you again. Not ever."

GWEN LET THE fervor of his words strengthen her. If anyone understood what she'd been through, it was Luke. He'd lost everything right alongside her. And when she'd asked him to, he'd had the grace to let her go, as well.

She dunked half a fry in the paper cup of ketchup at the edge of her plate and tried desperately to relax. But so much had changed. Her. Him. *Them.* He didn't even go by his nickname anymore. The female officer had nearly laughed when Gwen had requested to speak with Luke Winchester.

"Are you doing okay?" he asked, concern marring his handsome brow.

"Not really," she admitted. Being back in West Liberty was harder than she'd expected, and so was seeing him.

He'd aged unfairly well, of course, filled out in all the right places and seemed impossibly more fit than he had in college. He carried himself differently now, too, no longer the dorky future architect she'd fallen in love with. This Luke, *Lucas*, she corrected herself, had a coolness in his eyes and tension to his limbs she'd never known in him. "You've barely touched your beer."

"The night's young," he said, absently, his gaze searching the crowd.

"Is it? Or are you on duty right now?" she asked. "Because you seemed agitated when we sat down, now you're clearly on edge."

His lips curled into a cocky grin. "I don't know what you mean."

"Don't do that," Gwen snapped, the words coming more harshly than she'd intended. She pulled her shoulders back and pressed her lips together briefly before going on. "Don't pretend like I don't know you. You're scanning the crowd on a regular circuit, and you've angled yourself on the bench for a better look at the door and front window. You're obviously on alert, and if it's because of what I told you, I need to know. The fact that you're nursing that beer makes me think you want to keep a clear head, and I worry that it's because you think what I've told you is cause for concern and that I might be in danger."

He swiveled forward, eyes hot and jaw locked. "I don't know if you're in danger. I didn't even know you lived twenty minutes away until thirty minutes ago, but for what it's worth, yeah. I think you were smart to trust your instincts. And I don't believe in coincidences."

Gwen's stomach rolled. The wine and french fries revolted in her gut. As they should have. She wasn't twenty-two and carefree anymore. This night was too much. The whole day was too much. She rubbed her fingertips against a napkin and pushed the plate aside. "I should probably use the ladies' room then head home."

Lucas stood silently and waited at the end of the table while she gathered her things and slid out.

"What about your sliders?"

"I'll get a box." He stretched one arm toward the hallway in the back of the pub, then trailed her as she made her way to the ladies' room.

The protective gesture warmed her heart and stung her eyes.

He leaned against the wall outside the restroom while she hurried inside.

She splashed cold water on her face, then ripped the pins and elastic from her hair, letting her curls fall free. She plucked the creamy fabric of her silk blouse away from her heated skin a few times, then dabbed a wet paper towel along her neck and collarbone. "You are safe," she told the wide brown-eyed reflection staring back at her. Lucas was clearly still perfect, impossibly sexier than she'd remembered and on her side. If there was anything to fear, he would let her know. Until then, she'd finger-comb her crazy hair, wipe the drops of water from her face and go home for some much needed sleep.

She reopened the bathroom door and Lucas smiled.

"Hey." He reached for her with an apologetic look in his eyes, and she nearly leapt into him. "I should've done this earlier," he whispered into her wild and unruly hair. His protective arms wound around her, tucking her in tight. "It's nice to see you, Gwen. You look stunning as always, and I'm glad you're here." He released her too soon, gripping her shoulders gently and fixing her with a determined gaze. "I don't know what's going on back in New Plymouth, but I meant what I said about protecting you any way I can. A lot of things have changed between us, but not that. Never that."

"Thanks."

He motioned her ahead of him, back through the crowd toward the table. "So, what happened in that bathroom?" he asked. "It looks like your hair went crazy."

"Shut up." She shot him a sideways look as they reached the booth. "I thought you always liked my crazy hair."

"I do." He scooped a disposable container off the

table. "I saw the waitress while I was waiting. She got the box ready."

"Great. Where's the bill?"

Lucas scanned the table and benches, then checked on the floor beneath. "I'll ask at the register."

Gwen led the way and stopped behind an older couple getting change. She slid her coat on as they waited, butterflies swooping in her core. Her nerves burned, hyperaware of Lucas's nearness and the way he made her feel when he looked at her like she wasn't permanently broken. She longed to reach for him again, hungry for the physical contact and proof she wasn't alone.

He smiled at the cashier as the older couple moved away, then explained where he'd been seated and requested the bill.

The younger woman smiled politely, then tapped on the register.

Gwen winced as the familiar tingles of paranoia lifted the fine hairs on her arms and neck. She scanned the room in search of someone looking her way, but the lively crowd was lost to itself, tuned in to a hundred different conversations that had nothing to do with her or her problems.

"It looks like your bill has been paid," the cashier said brightly.

"What?" Lucas asked. "By who?"

The uneasy sensation of being watched rode over Gwen's skin once more, and she clutched on to Lucas's sleeve for support.

"Are you sure you've got the right table?" Lucas

asked, a clear measure of disbelief in his tone. "We were alone in the corner booth."

"Positive," the cashier said pertly. "There's even a note in the register's memo. Must've been a friend. It says, 'Welcome Home.'"

Chapter Four

Lucas felt his jaw lock and his senses heightened. He reached for Gwen on instinct, setting a protective palm over her hand, resting on his sleeve. "Can you remember what the person who paid this bill looked like?" he asked, reaching into his pocket for the badge he rarely went anywhere without. "This is important, so think carefully." He presented the badge, and the cashier's eyes widened.

"No. It wasn't me," she said.

"Then who?" Lucas demanded. If he had a chance at finding this alleged friend, time was of the essence, and the cashier was wasting his.

"Uhm." She stared nervously at the cash register's computer screen, her round cheeks going red under pressure. "It was Thomas. Server nineteen." She looked up proudly and clearly relieved. "We use our codes to access the register."

"Where's Thomas now?" Lucas asked. "I need to speak with him."

"Okay." The young woman backed away from the

register and rose onto her toes. "He usually covers the back."

Gwen stepped closer, then sucked in a ragged breath, as if she'd temporarily forgotten to breathe.

"There!" the cashier said. "Tall. Black hair. Brown eyes." She thrust a hand over her head and waved. "Thomas!"

Lucas leaned his head closer to Gwen's while he tracked Thomas visually through the room. "You're all right," he promised her. "I've got you."

She nodded quickly and seemed to struggle to swallow.

Lucas flashed his badge again as Thomas approached.

The server was lean and young, likely just old enough to handle the alcohol he served. He'd threaded his way through the crowd with ease and agility. An athlete, likely. And based on his posture and expression, a cocky one.

Thomas cast a wary gaze at the girl behind the counter. "What's up?" he asked, dragging his attention from her to Lucas. "I do something wrong?"

"No." Lucas motioned to the register. "I'd like a description of the person who paid our bill."

Thomas stepped around to the register and examined the screen. "Corner booth. Sliders and fries." He looked up with a frown. "Sorry, man. I barely looked at that guy."

Not surprising on a night as busy as this. "How long ago did he pay?" Lucas asked. "Was it in cash? Did he use a card?" Lucas nearly snorted at the absurdity. If the bill-payer was up to no good, as suspected, he wouldn't have used a credit card. Unless it was stolen, or the user was stupid. Lucas wasn't that lucky.

And if they were truly dealing with Gwen's attacker, he wasn't that stupid.

"He gave me cash," Thomas said, projecting his voice above the crowd. "Maybe ten minutes ago. Told me to keep the change. I wish I could tell you more, but I can't, and it's crazy busy. Now, if you'll—"

"No," Lucas said, widening his stance and pressing his palm onto the counter between them. "I need a description of the man who paid this bill. You can tell me here or at the station."

Thomas smacked his lips. "Man, I didn't do anything wrong, but I'm about to be fired if I—"

"Get arrested?" Lucas asked. "Please, check the time stamp. I want to know how long ago this man was here. Did you see him leave?"

Thomas shook his head, forcing his attention back to the register. "Says seven twelve, and no, I didn't see him leave. In case you haven't noticed, this place is packed. I'm barely keeping up, and leaving my area to come up here and pay your bill pulled me away from my tables. Now, I'm up here again, and I can't help you."

Lucas glanced at his watch. Thomas had handled the bill nearly twenty minutes ago. Long enough for the person to be out of town by now. "Take a look around," Lucas said, scanning the bar. "Do you see him? Was he with anyone when you spoke to him?"

Thomas looked slowly around, his agitation turning to defeat. "Nah, man. I don't see him. He was alone near the dartboard in back when he stopped me. I was rushing past with a big order. He put a wad of cash on my tray, told me what he wanted me to do and I agreed. That was it. I served the table, then came up here to pay your bill. After that, I got back to work. There's nothing else to tell."

"He stopped you," Lucas repeated, "gave you more work to do, a task that wasn't your job and paid with a large sum of cash, but you can't tell me what he looked like? You don't know if he was Black or white? Hispanic or Asian? Short? Tall? Young? Old?"

"He was old, all right?" Thomas said. "Probably thirty. He looked like all of you, decked out in our gear, coming back here for homecoming and trying to relive your college years."

Lucas sucked his teeth and forced himself not to argue that he was twenty-eight, not thirty, and neither age was old. *Unless you were twenty-one*, he supposed. He took another look at the crush of bodies in the popular pub. Thomas was right. At least half were clearly over twenty-five and most were wearing Bellemont College colors or jerseys. They really did all look alike. He tipped his head to motion Thomas away from the register. "Got any security cameras in here?"

"Yeah." He lifted a finger to indicate a single unit above the cash register. A place the man who paid their bill had been careful not to go.

"Thanks," Lucas said, passing Thomas a few bucks for his time. Lucas had waited tables once, too, and he knew how important tips were to survival.

Gwen's grip on his arm loosened, and she backed

away. "What now?" she asked, shoving her hands into her pockets.

"Now, we get you home," Lucas said, scanning the crowd for anyone who seemed especially interested in them. "There's no one else to talk to here. We know whoever paid our bill didn't go to the register. And I've got no description, other than old." He slid a sideways look in her direction, and her lips curved up on one side.

"I don't think you're old," she said.

"That's because I've only got a year on you." He left his card on the counter with the cashier, then led Gwen back onto the sidewalk. "I think you should stay at my place tonight," he said, once they were free of the music and gonging mashup of sounds.

"I don't think so," she said. "I have work tomorrow morning, and I never miss. The last thing I need is to alert anyone at the office that something might be wrong."

He stifled the urge to remind her that something was definitely wrong, and she had no reason to try to hide it. "Then you should consider letting me stay with you. Either way, I don't think you should be alone tonight. We've confirmed you're being followed, and I'm willing to bet this guy isn't overjoyed to see you with another man, or a cop. Since I check both of those boxes, there could be a problem."

Gwen shivered. "We can go to my house."

Lucas drove Gwen back to the police station parking lot, then followed her home at precisely the speed limit. Him in his new extended cab black pickup with a local PD sticker in the window. Her in her nondescript, plain as hell gray sedan. They turned off the main road through her town and into an older neighborhood with compact, nearly utilitarian homes lining each side of every street. Cookie-cutter boxes with postage-stamp yards and limited privacy, short of shutting all the blinds.

Gwen's home was sandwiched between two white single-story cottages on a cul-de-sac. Hers was a cheery yellow number with white shutters, a red door and security cameras everywhere.

She pulled into the attached one-car garage, then motioned him to follow once he'd parked in the drive.

She ducked her head shyly when he met her in the small space, then pressed a button on the wall, closing the garage door before unlocking the door to her home.

Gwen turned the lock on the knob behind them, then flipped two dead bolts and secured a chain before entering a code to stop the wailing security alarm. She waited, frozen, staring at the screen until a row of green numbers appeared beside the word *SECURE*.

With the alarm silenced, Gwen headed for the kitchen. "Can I get you something? Water or coffee?"

"Water is fine," he said, taking a turn around the home's living space.

The decor was simple and tidy. White everything, with an occasional blue-patterned pillow, strategically placed silver centerpiece or a leafy green plant to break up the monotony. The result was attractive, intentional and devoid of personality. Like a magazine cover. Staged, but not lived in.

Each room opened to the next in a typical, continuous plan. The kitchen flowed into an eating space that spilled left into a family room and right into a formal dining area, which Gwen had set up as an office. The living room and office were connected by a small foyer and hall which he assumed led to the bedrooms. "You have a nice place."

"Thank you."

The sounds of cupboard doors, clinking glasses and jostling ice cubes drifted through the space to his ears.

"Everything here is original," she called. "It's got good bones, and I knew I had to have it the moment the Realtor pulled into the drive. The place needed a lot of TLC back then, but I've been diligent. Refinishing woodwork, repairing crown molding, cabinets and floors. Pretty much anything the previous owners didn't get to. It's been a great experience, and I'm nearly done."

Lucas nodded to himself as he returned to her. Home restoration was a great way to pass a lot of time alone. "You were going to be an engineer," he said, watching as she approached, a glass in each hand.

"Life happened," she said, remorsefully. "I was going to be a lot of things."

Like his wife, he thought, uselessly angry again at what the actions of one monster had done to two futures. "Thanks." He accepted the water and sipped.

Gwen returned to the kitchen and stopped at an old landline telephone and answering machine combo. She pressed a blinking button on the answering machine, and a mechanical voice announced two new messages.

"Hello," a female voice greeted. "This is Dr. Maslow's office calling to confirm your appointment—"

Gwen pressed another button, moving quickly to the next message.

"Hey. Gwen. It's Collin," a friendly man's voice said. "I was thinking about that rain check and wondering what you think of dinner at—"

Gwen interrupted the second message like the first. She glanced at Lucas, looking suddenly as uncomfortable in her home as she had in the bar.

"You keep a landline?" Lucas asked. "Not a popular convention these days." Though he suspected he knew why it appealed to Gwen. Landlines were more reliable than cell phones when calling for emergency services, and a cell signal blocker couldn't stop a landline call. For someone still recovering emotionally from an attack, like Gwen clearly was, a secondary form of communication probably seemed wise. Comforting, at least.

Her cell phone hadn't helped her before.

"The landline came with the house." She shrugged. "It's convenient and always charged. Plus I never have to go hunting for it."

"All true," Lucas said, then watched as her smile faded, having never truly reached her eyes.

"And the security system uses it."

He set his water aside, thoughts running back to the messages that had been waiting for her. "You have a doctor's appointment. Are you feeling okay?"

"Therapist," she said softly. "I started seeing someone again a few weeks ago when the feelings of being watched grew unusually persistent. I thought I was relapsing. It was scary."

"Understandable," Lucas said. "You were smart to set up the appointments. Everyone needs someone to talk to." He tried not to wonder who her confidant was now, and if she talked to the man from the messages the way she used to talk to him.

Gwen climbed onto a stool at the kitchen island and cradled her glass between her palms. "Go on. Ask whatever you need to. I want to help you figure out what's going on here, however I can. It's been a while since I opened up about my life, but I'm going to do my best. I know it's important that you get all the facts, and that I'm as honest as possible with my answers. We need to know who's following me and why."

He took the seat beside her and tapped his thumbs against the table's edge. "How many people know where you live?" he began. "How many have been here? And how many of them have come inside with you after being away?"

"How many people have seen me disable my alarm?" she asked. "How many might have memorized the code as I typed it? None."

"Good," he said. "How many have been inside, seen your layout and the security measures in place?"

"Three," she said easily, releasing her glass in favor of crossing her arms. "My mother, my father and Marina from my office."

Lucas felt his brows raise. "In all the years since you moved in, only three people have come over to visit?"

"Yes."

"Okay. What about neighbors and friends? Anyone you've told about your attack or your recent feelings of being followed? Anyone your stalker might go to for information on you? Or someone he might use as a way to hurt you?"

Her eyes widened slightly, but she didn't flinch. "No. Everyone on my street keeps to themselves, and I'm not especially close to anyone. I don't talk about what I've been through outside of therapy. There's no reason to relive it more than I already do, and I don't want the pity that inevitably comes when people learn that I'm a victim."

"Were," Lucas said, feeling the familiar knot of regret and empathy in his core.

"What?"

"You were a victim. Once. Six years ago. You aren't a victim anymore," he assured her. He wouldn't allow her to be.

Gwen's lips tugged into a small, sad smile. "You're wrong."

"I'm not," he said, resolve rising in him. He hadn't been able to stop her from becoming a victim before, but that was a lifetime ago, in a world where they were getting married and he was going to be an architect. Her attacker had shattered those dreams, and Lucas was left alone to pick up the pieces. He made a damn good special victim's detective from the rubble, and he was going to make sure Gwen's stalker regretted ever targeting her.

Chapter Five

Gwen woke before dawn, eager to get outside for a run. She swung her feet out from beneath her covers, and the events of the previous day rushed back to her with a snap.

There wouldn't be a run in the park this morning. Not with someone following her, and Luke Winchester in her guest room. *Lucas*, she reminded herself once more. He went by Lucas now. A more grown-up name for the more grown-up man. One with all the heart and compassion she'd once loved, packed into a more-mature and slightly brooding, but equally attractive, package.

She rubbed her forehead to clear her thoughts, then shuffled toward her dresser in search of an outfit. Having Lucas in the next room, in her new life, was confusing and complicated enough without thinking about his handsome face or soulful eyes. Never mind the intense compassion he still had in spades. Her addled, sleepy mind thought that maybe being near him again was worth the tension of being followed for a little while.

A good sign she needed coffee. And a run.

Lucas had fallen in love with a whimsical young

college student, and Gwen was officially an uptight, no-nonsense hermit. The attraction these days could only run one way. She was lucky he'd agreed to help at all after she'd shown up at his precinct, without invitation or notice.

Gwen dressed for a date with her treadmill, then headed to the kitchen for some much-needed caffeine.

"Morning," Luke said, startling her as she exited her bedroom. His smile was warm and his hair mussed. He was dressed nearly identical to her, in black running pants and matching long-sleeved top. "I keep a gym bag in my truck," he said, apparently noticing her staring. "Sometimes I work out at the precinct."

"Yeah, you do," she muttered, allowing herself a moment to appreciate his broad shoulders, flat stomach and long, lean legs. She easily imagined what his body must look like under those clothes, clinging in all the right places.

His lips kicked up on one side and he chuckled. "I thought we could have breakfast, then maybe go for a run."

"Okay," she said, unsure when he'd begun running, but liking the idea.

"I can drop you off at work afterward, then I'll head back to West Liberty and take care of things there. I can be back to your office in time to drive you home."

Gwen tensed, all the warm and fuzzy feelings going cold. "You can't drive me to work. People will see you. What am I supposed to say?"

"That a friend dropped you off? Your car is in the

shop?" he suggested. "Everyone's ride needs maintenance eventually."

She considered the simple response. Car maintenance. It sounded completely logical coming from him, but no one had ever driven her to work, and she wasn't convinced she could so easily explain it away. "I want to think about it."

"Sure. How about some oatmeal and coffee before we go?" he motioned her toward the kitchen, and she led the way.

The scent of fresh-brewed coffee drifted out to greet her. Two mugs waited beside a full pot and a bowl of mixed fruits.

"I hope you don't mind," Luke said. "I cut up some of your melon. The berries and grapes looked as if they needed to be eaten before they went bad. I thought the cantaloupe was a good addition."

"Not at all." Gwen smiled, recalling all the times he'd made her breakfast in another life. Usually burnt pancakes or hurried scrambled eggs before class. "Thank you." She poured coffee into both mugs, then spooned up two bowls of fresh fruit.

Lucas lifted a teakettle from her stove as it began to sing and added the steaming water to bowls of dried oats. He topped the mixture with brown sugar and drizzled it with maple syrup, then ferried the finished products to the island.

"Wow." Gwen took a seat. "This is fantastic," she said, popping a strawberry chunk into her mouth. It had been years since she'd had breakfast with someone, or eaten more than whatever she could grab on her way out the door. "You're really going to run with me?"

"If you don't mind," he said, sipping gingerly at his coffee. "I'll try to keep up."

She rolled her eyes and tried again not to think about his body or his incredible kindness. He'd made her breakfast and wanted to drive her to work. It was as if her past and present were colliding, and Gwen wasn't prepared to handle the emotions that came with that.

AN HOUR LATER, Lucas stood, winded, in Gwen's kitchen, having escorted her on a reconnaissance run through the neighborhood. She'd pointed out every home belonging to someone she knew, as well as those that had been recently purchased. Lucas made a note of those standing empty, either awaiting a renter or up for sale, but nothing had struck him as odd or problematic. Nothing had set off any textbook red flags or triggered his gut instinct, and that was the real problem. Because something *was* wrong. Gwen was being followed on her runs, to her office and almost assuredly to her home.

"When did you become a runner?" Gwen asked, swigging water from her bottle and wiping sweat from her brow.

Lucas shrugged, pulling himself back to the moment. "A few years ago." He'd had trouble sleeping after Gwen's attack. Hellacious nightmares. When she'd left, he struggled with internal rage and self-loathing. He'd needed a healthy outlet, one that didn't involve booze or women. "You always said it helped you think and get centered. I gave it a try and have to agree."

She nodded, then smiled. "I'm glad it helped."

The smile reached her eyes and did things to his heart rate. "You should probably catch that shower so you aren't late for work. I'd hate to make you late on my first drop-off mission."

Gwen glanced at the clock, then moved quickly away. "I won't be long," she called.

He laughed as she darted into the bathroom down the hall. "You always say that," he called back. "It's never true."

He gripped the back of his neck, hard. Reminding himself for the hundredth time to remember his place. Gwen didn't need a boyfriend or even a buddy. She needed protection. She was in danger, and he couldn't afford to let his guard down the way he had before. Never again. Last time, she'd nearly been killed.

He refilled his water bottle with the pitcher in her fridge, then paused to examine a set of snapshots he hadn't noticed before. A small collection of selfies was lined up like soldiers on a corkboard near the pantry. A shot of Gwen's parents. One of Gwen at her high school graduation. The family dog, Jeeves. And a photo of Gwen in Lucas's arms, taken at their engagement party.

His eyelids slid shut with the bittersweet memory of that moment, and pressure built in his chest. Their engagement had been the happiest moment of his life, and within forty-eight hours, his heart had been ripped from his chest. The smiling, youthful faces in that image had no idea how bad things were about to get, and he wished for the thousandth time that he could go back and warn them.

He'd proposed on Friday night, Homecoming Weekend, and they'd spent the next day or so in bed, celebrating. By Sunday, however, she couldn't wait to show the ring off and announce the news to all of her friends. When she was late coming home, Lucas hadn't worried. When she didn't answer her phone, he assumed it was loud wherever she was and she hadn't heard it ring. Or maybe she'd had an extra margarita and fallen asleep at a friend's place. When he'd gone to bed alone that night, she was being beaten and raped. When he'd fallen asleep under the covers, safe and content, she'd been naked and alone, fighting for her life and counting the moments, in and out of consciousness until dawn.

Lucas had never once worried for her safety.

No thanks to him, she'd lived, but she'd come through it into another life. One that hadn't included room for a man, and he couldn't blame her. But he also couldn't help finding hope in the single photo she'd kept of them. Maybe Gwen didn't blame him as completely for what happened to her as he did.

"I'm glad you're here," she said, high heels snapping against hard wood as she hurried back down the hall in his direction. She'd dressed in a cream blouse and black skirt with a string of pearls her mother had given her on her twenty-first birthday, the night he realized he wanted to marry her.

"Glad to be here," he said, feigning casualness and reminding himself not to reach for her as she approached. A habit he had to unlearn. "You look great."

"Thanks." She'd twisted her wild red curls into an updo again and had a pair of simple gold hoop earrings in her hand. "I'm sure it speaks volumes about my emotional state, but I'm glad you agree with me about someone following me. Knowing I'm right feels slightly better than thinking I'm losing my mind." She offered a small smile as she plugged a hoop into one ear, then another. "Being alone all the time is one thing. I'm not willing to let go of my sanity just yet, too."

"You're far from crazy," he said, meeting and holding her gaze. "You went through the unthinkable, and you created a new life for yourself afterward. A very carefully designed and executed life. To think the danger you've worked so hard to put behind you could be here and now?" He gave a short humorless laugh. "Let's just say I can appreciate how surreal it is when two timelines collide."

She blinked, then dipped her chin and turned away. "We should get going."

Lucas cringed, having clearly said the wrong thing. Unsure how to make it better instead of worse, he kept his mouth shut and followed her into the day. He waited while she set the alarm and locked her multitude of locks, then he walked her to his truck.

He opened her door and waited while she climbed inside. He admired her strength and will. She'd gotten through the most horrible thing he could imagine a person going through, and she'd done it on her own. Her terms. Her choices. Her success. She might not be in his life anymore, but he was still incredibly proud of her. And willing to do whatever he could to help her find peace again.

"We will figure this out," he promised, pausing before he closed her door. "And for whatever it's worth, you aren't alone, Gwen. Not anymore."

Chapter Six

Gwen climbed down from Lucas's truck with a promise not to leave her office building under any circumstances, and he vowed to be back for her at six sharp. It was a strange feeling, having another human in her immediate orbit again. Someone who made her breakfast, went running with her and drove her to work. It was something she hadn't experienced in a long time, and she was surprised how deeply she'd missed it.

He watched her walk inside before pulling away from the curb.

Marina waited silently inside the glass doors kneading her hands and nearly buzzing with excitement. "Who was that?" she asked, eyes wide as she followed Gwen across the foyer. "Did you meet him at the park?"

Gwen smiled as evenly as possible, ignoring the swarm of butterflies taking flight in her chest. "That was Lucas."

Debbie watched from her position at the elevators as they approached. She pressed the Up button and turned to Gwen with a cat-that-ate-the-canary grin on her face. "Morning," she said sweetly. "I didn't realize you were seeing anyone, Gwen. When did this begin? And does Collin know?"

Marina moved to Debbie's side, and the two of them waited for Gwen's answer.

"I'm not seeing him," Gwen answered. "We've known one another a long time, and why would I tell Collin if I was seeing someone?"

The pair exchanged a look, then rolled their eyes in near unison.

"So, why the ride to work?" Marina asked. "Everything okay?"

The elevator doors parted, and Gwen rushed inside. "My car's in the shop. I'm getting some basic maintenance and needed a ride."

"Will he be taking you home tonight, too?" Debbie asked, their reflections staring back in the shiny elevator walls as they rose to their floor.

"Yep."

"Will we get to meet him?" she asked.

The doors opened, and Gwen made her escape. "Maybe. I'll see you guys soon. I've got to call the shop and make sure they know where I left the key," she said, speed-walking toward her office as the other women stopped to chat with the receptionist.

She ducked into her small sanctuary and shut the door, then did her best to keep her head down until her stomach demanded it was lunchtime.

At twelve thirty, she opened her bag and groaned. She forgot to pack a lunch, and she'd promised Lucas she wouldn't go out.

A small sound drew her attention to the window

behind her. When the noise came again, she turned slowly in her chair to stare at the glass. Something small bounced off and she started. A pebble or maybe an acorn? Someone was throwing things at her window? Someone knew which window was hers?

Her muscles stiffened and her breath caught as she waited to see if it happened again.

Tink! Another pebble.

Tink! A pebble.

Thump!

A stone hit the window, and the glass rattled.

Gwen jumped in her chair. Her heart hammered as she pressed onto her feet and maneuvered in a wide arc through the room, coming up alongside of her window. She swallowed long and slow, then dared a peek outside.

"Gwen?" The receptionist's voice burst through the speaker on her desk phone.

Gwen yelped. She pressed her back to the wall and a palm against her aching chest. She stumbled forward and pressed the response button on her phone. "Yes?" she croaked, forcing the word past a massive lump in her throat.

"You have a delivery."

Ice slid through her veins and pooled in her stomach. "I didn't order anything."

She turned back to the window, fearful of who was below and what she might find if she looked. But she had to look. Had to know. If someone was really targeting her, trying to terrorize her, she had to help Lucas make the arrest. If she didn't, this might never end. And if she found some other reasonable explanation for the pebbles hitting her window, then she could relax and figure out what to do about lunch.

She squared her shoulders and crossed the room, determined to see something other than a stalker. She took a deep breath and peered into the lot below.

No one was there.

She fell back against the wall, breathing heavily and shaking slightly. No one was there, but someone had been. Hadn't they?

Was her stalker getting braver? Bolder? Angrier? Had he seen her with Lucas?

If her coworkers were this worked up about her ride to work, what did her stalker think? Did he also know Lucas had spent the night? Realizing how bad that would look from the outside, she felt her empty stomach roll. Apprehension gripped her shoulders and tightened the muscles in her neck and core.

"Miss Kind?" An unfamiliar male voice spoke behind her and she squelched a scream.

A man in jeans and a leather jacket crossed the room to her desk with a large bag in one hand. The receptionist held the door open for him.

He unearthed a massive plastic container filled with salad from the bag and placed it on her desk, then added a baguette, bottle of water and an apple to the arrangement. "Enjoy." He shot her an uncomfortable look, then headed back the way he'd come.

"You okay?" the receptionist asked, lingering in the threshold and looking more than a little concerned.

"Mmm-hmm." Gwen forced her hand from her chest and nodded. "I didn't order lunch. That's all."

"There's a note," she said. "Let me know if you need anything." She closed the door on her way out, leaving Gwen alone once more.

She moved to the desk and tugged the note free from the container.

Now you don't need to go out.
See you at 6.
Lucas.

She collapsed into her chair with a smile and shook her head at the nonsense she'd put herself through. No one was throwing pebbles at her second-floor window. And even if someone was, they were gone now, and she wasn't alone anymore. She had Lucas, and she was going to count her blessing on that fact every minute until her personal nightmare was over.

THE OFFICE EMPTIED quickly at five o'clock. A few coworkers had joked about waiting for a look at Gwen's ride home, but thankfully no one had been willing to wait an extra hour. Gwen bit into her apple, having saved the sweet treat for exactly this moment. A nice reminder that even when Lucas wasn't physically with her, she still wasn't alone.

Collin appeared outside her open door and smiled, redirecting his path. "You've been busy," he said, stepping into the doorway and leaning casually against the jamb. "I was going to see if you were hungry at lunch today, but word around the office is that you got delivery."

"I did." She set the bitten apple on her desk and pressed her lips into a smile. "Rain check?" she asked, regretting the words immediately. She didn't want a rain check. Her neatly arranged world didn't have room for rain checks or plans of any sort. Especially now. The fewer people who were dragged into her mess, the better.

"Sure thing." Collin winked. "But I've got to tell you, those rain checks are adding up. Pretty soon you're going to have to cash them in for dinner. Or a pony."

Gwen laughed. "I've always wanted a pony."

Collin hung his head and mimed stabbing himself in the chest as he walked away.

Her smile lingered as she went back to her apple.

Almost five thirty, and Lucas would be back for her soon. Her bag was packed and waiting at her feet. Until then, she dared an internet search for recent attacks at Bellemont College. There were plenty of minor incidents and the usual reports of male-on-female crimes, but nothing like what she'd experienced.

She enjoyed the sweet crunch of her snack as she performed a wider search, broadening the parameters from the college to the community, then the city and county.

A door slammed somewhere in the quiet building, and she jolted upright.

A chorus of voices arrived with the elevator, blurring into gibberish before being drowned out by the sounds of vacuum cleaners.

The cleaning crew.

Gwen turned to her window, peering into the parking lot for confirmation.

The rear door to her building was propped open, and two uniformed women chatted while unloading trays of cleansers and carts of supplies.

She breathed easier, then returned to her desk as her phone buzzed with an incoming text.

On my way. Running late. See you soon.

She pushed the rest of her apple into the trash and rested her head in her hands for a long beat, regaining her composure and reminding herself she was safe.

Lucas's words returned to her from the night before. He'd said she wasn't a victim anymore, but the truth was that she'd never stopped being one. Her attack had changed her. Had altered her very being. And afterward, she'd built a nice, safe life around herself in an active attempt to keep the monster at bay.

And now, he was back.

The vacuums and voices fell silent at six o'clock.

Gwen wiped a tear she hadn't realized was forming. Her shaking hands were white-knuckled and curled into fists she hadn't meant to make.

Outside, an engine revved to life, and she breathed easier. The cleaning crew was leaving.

Her phone buzzed, and she nearly wept with relief when she saw it was Lucas.

I'm here. Building's locked. Have a good day?

Yep

She pried her body from the chair and collected her bag.

On my way.

She opened her office door and froze.

The dimmed space around her was charged with an uncomfortable energy. Her instincts rose to attention, reaching out, trying to place the source of the alarm.

Then she heard it. A continuous, muffled sound that scattered goose bumps across her skin and rooted her feet into place. She dialed Lucas.

"Hey," he answered. "Sorry I was running late. There was an accident on—"

"Shh," she whispered, feeling the panic twist and grind inside her. "Something's wrong. I think someone's here."

Lucas didn't respond for a long beat. "What's the security code for the building?" he asked.

She recited the numbers quickly, then stepped back into her office.

Images of sliding down the wall into a sobbing heap on the floor crossed her mind. Shoving her desk against the locked door. Even jumping from her window. Anything to stop her former attacker from getting his hands on her again. She'd die first.

No, she thought, suddenly, forcing the desperation from her head. *No.* She'd worked hard to vanquish those kinds of thoughts. To recover. To heal. Her lips trembled as she recalled the sleepless nights spent in a ball on her closet floor. Hiding. Crying. Praying he'd never find her. And how she'd finally vowed to stop letting him control her.

Gwen grabbed the large pewter Employee of the Year award from her credenza and gripped it like a baseball bat.

She was done running.

Done giving this psycho all the little pieces of herself one by one.

She marched toward the sounds. Down the narrow hall separating offices from conference rooms, the mail room and employee lounge. She stopped outside the only closed door in the office and steeled her waning resolve. Whatever was going on, it was happening in the mail room.

"Gwen!" Lucas called. His voice arriving with the ding of the elevator. "Gwen!"

"Here!" she called back.

He halted at her side a moment later, drawing his weapon and tucking her behind him as he opened the mail room door.

Inside, the massive corporate copy machine chugged and spewed its paper contents. Sheet by sheet across the floor.

A thousand photos of Gwen.

All recent and surveillance-style.

Chapter Seven

Thirty minutes later, Lucas paced through Gwen's office while she relayed the details of her situation to a local detective and a pair of officers processed the copier.

"And that's everything," Gwen said, having held her composure through a retelling of her past that made Lucas want to scream.

Special Victims Detective Heidi Anderson perched primly in a chair across from Gwen's desk. Her sleek blond hair hung neatly around her face, tucked behind her ears and barely reaching her shoulders. "And you believe the person who printed the photos tonight is the same man who attacked you six years ago?" she asked, sharp brown eyes narrowing behind dark-rimmed glasses.

"It's just a guess," Gwen answered. "Whoever it is, he knows where I work and jog, and that I went to Belle-mont College. I suppose it's possible that someone else is doing this. Maybe someone on the periphery of my current life has become obsessed. I'd actually prefer that," she said with a sad smile. "Because I know what my attacker is capable of."

The detective dipped her chin in understanding. "I'm very sorry."

Gwen nodded back acceptance, then released a shuddered breath and pressed on. "Unfortunately, I can't link anything to my assailant. Aside from the location of the attack, all he left behind was an ugly aftermath."

Detective Anderson nodded. "I understand. And you reached out to Detective Winchester after you found the flyer on your windshield?" she clarified. "Because the attack was in his town and the college on the flyer is also in his jurisdiction?"

Gwen looked to Lucas before answering.

Detective Anderson arched a brow. "Was it something more?"

"Yes," Gwen said, and Lucas stilled. "We were engaged at the time of my attack."

The detective looked from Gwen to Lucas, then back. "I see. But you aren't together now."

"No."

"But you've remained close," she guessed.

Gwen shifted on her chair. "No." She folded her hands on the desk before her and stared at them. "I contacted Lucas when I found the flyer because he knows what happened to me, and until right now, I've never told anyone other than family, law enforcement and medical personnel. Anyone who read about it in the paper back then has surely forgotten about it, along with the first responders and medical staff who cared for me. I don't keep in touch with the friends I had then.

So, aside from my parents, Lucas is the only one who would understand why I thought a simple homecoming invitation might be a threat."

The frank and emotionless assessment hit Lucas like a cold fist to his gut, and he reeled at the response. He'd known the words were true, but hearing her say them gave him an unexpected pause. Gwen had come to him last night because she had no one else to go to. Not because she trusted him to protect her and to get her through this. Not because she wanted to see him again. Or because they'd always made a phenomenal team. But because she'd been avoiding this very situation. She hadn't wanted to talk about what she'd been through, and with Lucas, she didn't have to.

Detective Anderson uncrossed, then recrossed her legs. "Any chance this has anything to do with you?" she asked, moving her gaze to Lucas. "SVU detective's fiancée goes through something like you described, and I've got to ask, could her attack have been motivated by an angry criminal you collared?"

"I was a student at the time," Lucas said, clearing his throat when the words came thick and gravelly. "I joined the academy after her attack, when the local PD came up empty-handed."

She cocked her head and frowned. "So, after going through something like that, you decided to make a career out of it?"

"No," Lucas said sharply. "Not like that."

"Well, it wasn't for the glory or the money," she said, a remorseful lilt to her tone.

"I wanted to find the man who did this," he said. "I

wanted revenge and justice and some assurance that he'd never hurt anyone else or Gwen ever again."

Gwen covered her mouth, eyes glistening with unshed tears.

"He's still out there, but I've helped put plenty of others like him away," Lucas said. "And I'm not finished with this guy yet."

"Hmm." Detective Anderson looked from Lucas to Gwen. "I think I have everything I need." She closed the notebook she'd been making notes in. "I'll be in touch once the fingerprints from the mail room and copier are run and we've scanned the security feed from the parking lot cameras."

"The parking lot," Gwen whispered. She spun to face Lucas, eyes wide. "Someone was outside my window before lunch. Throwing pebbles and acorns, then a rock. I convinced myself I'd imagined it after looking and finding no one out there, but maybe someone was here."

Lucas nodded.

"Detective Anderson?" A man's voice turned everyone toward the door. One of the officers from the mail room stepped inside. "We found a thumb drive in the copier's USB port." He held a small evidence bag between his thumb and first finger.

"Excellent," she said, rising to her feet. "Then maybe we'll get some answers." She extended a hand to Gwen, then Lucas. "Ms. Kind, Detective," she said. "I'll be in touch. Please keep me posted if anything else comes up."

"Of course." Lucas shook her offered hand. "Thank you."

GWEN WATCHED AS Lucas crossed the space from her kitchen to her living room, delivering a steaming mug of tea to her hands. She'd curled on her couch, tucked her feet beneath her and pulled a pillow onto her lap, unable to do more than stare. "Thanks," she whispered. Her feeble attempts to process the evening had failed repeatedly. Nothing made any sense anymore. Least of all the fact that her carefully and tightly constructed world was suddenly unraveling.

Lucas took a seat on the cushion beside her and watched as she sipped her tea. "I think you should consider taking the rest of the week off work," he said. "Your boss knows what went on tonight. Detective Anderson spoke with her earlier. I think you could use the time to focus on what's happening."

"I know," Gwen said, instantly recalling the humiliation she'd felt listening to the detective's call. She'd been discreet in her words, but had made it clear, nonetheless, that the intended victim was Gwen. And there were no secrets in her office.

She had plenty of unused vacation time, and she wasn't in any hurry to face Marina or Debbie. They'd seen Lucas's truck this morning when he'd dropped her off, and likely noted the police shield sticker on the back window. They'd make the connection between her trouble and her protector. And there would be questions. "I'll call the office tomorrow," she agreed. "I'm sure they'll understand."

Lucas raised his brows. "Yeah?"

"Yeah."

He rubbed his palms against his thighs and a small smile formed. "I'd expected a fight."

"Sorry." She sighed. "I'm fresh out of fight. At least for tonight."

His expression turned soft, and he clasped his hands on his lap.

"Don't," she warned, shooting him a look over the rim of her mug. She'd seen that look before on a dozen people, and she hated it. "Don't you dare pity me. I'm just tired, and I'll be fine tomorrow."

"I don't pity you," he said, his tone gentle enough to break her. "I meant what I said before. You aren't a victim anymore, Gwen. I saw it the moment I set eyes on you in my precinct. You're a fighter. And I'm here to fight with you."

"I'm not a fighter," she said, wishing he was right, but feeling the defeat of exhaustion slipping over her.

"Really?" He laughed. "Because it wasn't two hours ago I found you with some kind of silver vase on your shoulder, ready to take out whoever was on the other side of your mail room door."

Gwen laughed, surprised by his words and at herself in the memory. "That was my Employee of the Year award, not a vase."

Lucas grinned.

"I just want this to end," she said. Frustration and fatigue warred in her, but her mind wouldn't let her sleep, not yet, even if she tried. Her stomach growled, and she knew she'd have to deal with that first. "Are you hungry?" They'd missed dinner thanks to the lunatic trying to scare her.

"A little," Lucas said. "But there's something else I want to run by you." He inched closer and pierced her with a sincere and hopeful gaze. "I think we should stay at my place through the weekend. Get out of town. This guy is getting bolder, and it worries me. I can protect you here, if he manages to get to you, somehow, but if we're at my place, we might be able to avoid that scenario completely. Focus on figuring out who he is, then go after him instead of the other way around."

Gwen gripped the bunching muscles in her shoulders and along her neck. She hadn't spent the night anywhere else in years. Her home was safe and familiar. Her life was composed of closed-circuit routes and routines that were easy to monitor and guard. Or so she'd thought. "Can I take a shower and think about it?" she asked, smiling when he grinned. She'd made a similar request earlier, and thankfully, he'd agreed.

Her need to consider everything thoroughly probably seemed odd to someone whose career required him to make split-second decisions, but for Gwen, thinking things through provided a layer of assurance she needed. She could have and should have gotten a ride home, like her friends had, on the night of her attack, but she'd refused. She was so naively filled with joy and promise that she'd chosen to walk home on a whim. She wanted to enjoy the crisp fall air, distant sounds of parties and laughter, and bask in the fact that her life was utterly perfect, on a beautiful campus, under the stars. And she had for a while. If only she'd taken time to think about the potential consequences…

She pushed onto her feet without waiting for Lucas's

response, then made her way down the hall, her eyes already on fire with the sting of rising tears.

GWEN STEPPED BACK into the hallway an hour later. Scents of rich, salty cheese and warm, buttery bread rose to meet her. She'd let herself have the breakdown she needed under the stream of hot water, and imagined the heartbreak, the fear and desperation circling the drain at her feet. She gave in to the feelings under her terms, and she let them go on her terms, as well. Down the drain beside her tears. She'd emerged from the shower with renewed resolve, with purpose and with hope.

Now, in her softest jeans and coziest sweater, wild curls swelling around her face as they dried, she padded toward her kitchen on socked feet. Toward the handsome man whistling at her stove. "Twice in one day?" she asked, sliding onto a stool at her island to admire the view.

Lucas cast an odd look over his shoulder. He flicked the knob on her stove, extinguishing the fire, then removed a perfect grilled cheese sandwich from the skillet. "Don't you normally eat more than once a day?"

"Yeah," she laughed, "but I make it myself."

He cut the sandwich into triangles and slid them onto a plate. "I was starting to worry about you in there. You were gone a while. I figured I'd keep myself busy while I waited."

Concern darkened his eyes as he delivered the plate to her.

"I'm fine," she lied. "Just taking my time."

He turned back to her stove, stirring the contents of

a small pot. "You still like tomato soup," he said, before pouring the smooth scarlet mixture into a bowl. "You've got a shelfful in your pantry."

"It's warm food on cold nights," she said. Plus, it reminded her of home. "My mom still makes and cans her own. Once upon a time a grilled cheese and tomato soup combo was the cure for all that ailed me." In fact, the soup reminded her so much of her mother, and how badly she missed her, that she had a hard time leaving the grocery without buying a can. And an even harder time making it for the same reason. Tears did nothing to enhance the flavor.

"Do your folks get up this way much?" Lucas asked, slipping a spoon and bowl before her.

"A few times a year." She smiled at the food. "I visit them for Christmas. How's your family?"

"Crazy," he said, rolling his eyes. "Blaze is still pining away for the woman he helped put into witness protection. It would be comical if it wasn't so sad. Derek's cocky as ever. Isaac's trying to heal the world, one patient at a time, and Mom is still trying to marry us all off. So far, we're sorely disappointing her." His expression flattened. "Same old."

Gwen turned her attention to the soup, stroking a spoon through the bowl's creamy contents. "Thanks for taking care of me today," she said, the words coming more softly than intended. "Part of me wants to be sorry I dragged you into this, because honestly, I was hoping you'd look at that flyer and tell me I was being completely paranoid. But I'm glad I asked."

"Because I was already familiar with the case?"

His keen blue eyes flicked to hers, something like hurt flashing in them.

"Because you're the only person I trust to not treat me as if I'm broken," she said. "Because you know what this monster has done to me and what he's taken from me. You've seen the scars." She stopped, pressing her lips tight and forcing her hands into her lap. Her fingers ached to reach for the scars on instinct. To be sure they were still there. And that the wounds were healed. Because sometimes she was sure the memories and phantom pains would kill her yet.

She'd needed dozens of stitches where her attacker had dug a blade into her side, and where he'd curled his fingers into her hair then banged her head repeatedly against the ground. Where doctors had painstakingly removed pebbles from her punctured skin and lacerated scalp. "I came to you because you know," she repeated, her throat clamping down on the final word.

"I do," he said, looking ashamed and guilty. He set a hand on hers in her lap, and she flinched. "Sorry," he said, pulling quickly away, expression horrified. "I'm so sorry. I didn't mean to do that."

Shock turned to humiliation in her heart and soul as she realized her mistake and his. It had been so long since anyone had reached for her hand. Since anyone had touched her outside her parents' hugs. The move had startled her, and she'd flinched. That was on her.

He'd forgotten she was broken. That was on him.

Regardless of what she wanted, her attacker had taken something from her that she'd never get back, and Lucas deserved more than a few pieces of someone who'd never again be whole. Her stomach rolled, and her hunger vanished. "Um." She slid to her feet, emotions spiking and churning in her core. "I need to lie down. Do you mind if we stay here one more night?" she said, backing away. "We can go to your place tomorrow. I won't argue."

"Gwen." Lucas stood, eyes pleading and hands rising uselessly between them.

"I'll clean the kitchen tomorrow," she said. "Don't worry about it. You've done too much already." A small sob burst from her lips, and she pressed a palm to her mouth. "Good night."

And she turned for her bed at a jog.

Chapter Eight

Early the next morning, Gwen watched the familiar streets pass by in a town she'd avoided for five long years. She'd foregone her run and eaten toast with her coffee, all in an attempt to leave home before the sun rose. Now, it was just after breakfast time for everyone else, and she was back in her old college town, West Liberty. Flags in the school's colors hung from streetlamps, and banners proclaiming Bellemont pride clung to shop windows and storefronts. The rolling green hills of campus ebbed and flowed in the distance, beyond quaint, historic neighborhoods and rows of rental homes filled with students

There was an undeniable energy in the air. Contagious and wild. Rosy-cheeked students with backpacks and steaming cups laughed on street corners and held hands on sidewalks. It was surreal and otherworldly. A movie set come to life. The picture of Midwestern collegiate perfection, where all days were good ones and monsters didn't lurk.

Nostalgia twitched and stretched in her core, calling on her good memories in this town. Of shared coffees and jokes between friends. But she shut it down, unable to recall the good without the bad, and unwilling to relive the bad.

"What did your boss say when you called in this morning?" Lucas asked, turning to her at a red light.

Gwen glanced his way, relieved for the distraction. "She understood. I asked for a week of vacation, but I don't see how that will be enough."

"I'll do everything I can to end this as soon as possible," he said. "If you need more time at the end of the week, we'll figure it out together. But let's take the days as they come for now."

The light changed, and they motored ahead, making turns down streets she remembered and others she couldn't recall.

Gwen didn't doubt his intent or motivation, but she suspected they needed more than a handful of days to find a man they hadn't been able to identify in six years. Assuming the current stalker was her old attacker, and she hadn't managed to attract a second lunatic.

Maybe it was time to put her home on the market and start over somewhere else. Farther away this time. Maybe Florida, near her folks. Though, she'd want to keep a little distance, just in case. She wouldn't want to put her parents in danger. Maybe she could buy a place a few towns over. Or not in Florida at all. A neighboring state.

"Gwen?" Lucas asked.

He'd been talking, she realized, and she'd missed whatever he'd said completely. "Sorry. What?"

He pressed his lips and shook his head. "You've

barely spoken since we left this morning. I asked, what are you thinking?"

She'd been thinking about how much she'd hate having to sell her home and give up her life again. How had it come to this when she'd worked so hard and been so careful? "I knew something wasn't right," she said, the thought flying from her mouth the moment it entered her head. "My instincts told me something was wrong, and I ignored them. And he'd been there. Did you see all those photos? He'd been everywhere. I was never alone. My carefully constructed life was all just a lie he'd allowed me to believe."

And she was a fool for having believed it.

"This is not your fault," Lucas said, pulling his truck into a narrow driveway. "There's no accounting for psychopathy. You're a sane person who made a sane decision based on a logical review of the evidence. Intuition can't trump facts when the facts were six years deep. No one this side of an asylum would have believed a man who'd nearly killed you once would be back now, quietly following you around." He cut the engine with a curse and climbed out of the cab.

Gwen blinked, mildly stupefied by his uncharacteristic loss of composure.

He opened her door looking chagrinned.

She slid onto her feet outside the truck. "Sorry. I guess I was feeling sorry for myself."

"You were blaming yourself. That's different." He pulled her bags onto his shoulders and shut her door. "The only one at fault here is the one committing the crimes." He smiled, dragging his gaze to the home beside them. "Welcome to my place. It's a work in progress."

Gwen turned to the house, finally seeing where he'd brought her. She sucked in a sharp breath and stared. "You bought the house?" she asked, nonsensically, the answer immediately in front of her.

"Yeah."

Lucas had bought the house she'd fallen in love with junior year. One they'd stood outside of a hundred times on their ways to and from local events and admired. One he'd vowed to buy her someday on the night he'd proposed.

"When?" she asked, thrilled for him and at the prospect of finally stepping inside.

The 1870 Gothic-revival home had caught her eye the first time she saw it. The stately brick structure was set back from the road and circled by an aged wrought iron fence. The arched windows and doorways were lined in ornate details and scrolling woodwork that had called to her. It was always on the market, overpriced for the amount of work that had to be done, but worth it, she'd thought, to own such a beautiful piece of history. The realty site had claimed it to be more than four thousand square feet of living space with five large bedrooms and a study. She'd imagined her children growing up there, running wild down halls and corridors, where children had played for nearly one hundred and fifty years before them.

"Last year," he said, answering her question.

He carried her bags onto the wide front porch and slid a key into the lock. "It took me longer to save the money on a cop's salary than it would have on an architect's, but I got it done." He pressed the door open and motioned her inside.

"But why?" she asked, hurrying to gape at the perfection around her. If the Realtor's website was a decent resource, the home had likely set him back by five times his annual salary, and it would take one full-time cop a lifetime to restore.

The grand entryway boasted high ceilings, hardwood floors and a chandelier. The staircase began at the back of the space and climbed to the next floor, its lacquered handrail gleaming from a recent polish.

She turned to him, desperate to know his reasoning. Senselessly hoping she'd been some small part of the decision, or at least the memory of her.

"I guess I'm still an architect at heart," he said. "My life might've taken an unexpected turn, but my dreams have never changed."

Her heart swelled at the implication left floating between them, and her body warmed with need for his touch.

"Come on. I'll show you the guest room." He started up the steps, and she followed.

Gwen trailed her fingertips along the banister and over fifty-year-old wallpaper as they climbed, admiring the refinished tread under her feet. The upstairs hallway was decorated the same. Perfect restored wooden floors and elaborate gilded paper. Crown moldings lined the ceilings and thick trim-rimmed doors and windows.

She peeked into the rooms as they passed, awed by the doors' original white porcelain knobs and craftsmanship. One bedroom acted as a home gym with a treadmill, weight set and mirror in place. Another posed as storage. A third seemed to be a home office. There was a desk and chair, but the boxes were also plentiful.

"This is the only other room with a bed," he said, stopping at the final door on his right, just past a bathroom. "I'll make it up for you. No one's ever actually needed it." He latched a hand on his hip and rubbed his forehead with the other. "You know what? Why don't you take my room instead? I'll figure this one out later."

He moved across the hall and pushed the door wide before Gwen could respond.

The room was huge with a massive four-poster bed at the center and evidence of Lucas's busy life everywhere. Toppled boots by the closet. Cast-off clothing on a chair. The scent of him trapped in every scrap of fabric and carpeting.

He dropped her bags on the bed, his gaze darting. "It's a mess, but at least there are sheets on the bed."

"It's great," she said, nodding to punctuate the words. "Thank you."

"Well then, I'll leave you to it." He slipped past her in the doorway, then paused in the hall. "I'm going to check in at the station and return some calls this morning. I won't be long, and we can get some lunch when I get back."

"You're leaving?" She spun on him, ripped back to the moment. "Take me with you. I want to know what's going on, and I can help."

"Gwen," he started, fixing a perfectly blank cop expression on his face. "I'll fill you in on everything when

I get back. I won't leave anything out. But I think you should stay inside as much as possible. I don't want you spotted, and honestly, there's no reason to drag you through the rehashing of details on this if we don't have to."

She crossed her arms, understanding his reasoning and hating it. "This is happening to me whether I want to deal with it or not, so I'm all in for the rehashing and whatever else it takes to catch him. I don't want to be left alone here, useless and idle. That'll only make me crazier." She stepped into the hall with him and leaned her head back for a look into his contemplative eyes. "Let me help you catch him this time."

Lucas clenched and released his jaw, the muscle flexing and jumping.

"Please?" she tried, taking another approach.

He groaned and rocked back on his heels, relenting. "All right. This way."

She followed him back toward the steps with an internal fist pump and a tiny kick in her step.

He stopped short at the room with a desk and chair, then flipped on the light. He waved a hand at the piles of boxes. "These are the details and findings from your original case, along with my personal research on the subject, not that I've ever gotten anywhere."

She inched into the room, surprised by his words. He'd told Detective Anderson that he'd put other monsters behind bars. It made sense for him to seek his justice however he could, and Gwen was glad he had. But knowing he'd kept hunting her attacker all these years was something else entirely. If he'd never given up on bringing her justice, then maybe he'd never given up on her. "Which boxes are the case files and research?" she asked. "Do you mind if I take a look?"

Lucas frowned. "These are all case files and research. Six years' worth."

"What?" Her heart pinched with appreciation and gratitude. While she'd been hiding, Lucas had been fighting. Her eyes stung, and she faked a yawn to cover the gathering tears.

She lifted the lid of the nearest box and peered inside. "I can't believe you have all these."

He leaned against the doorjamb, hands stuffed deep into the front pockets of his jeans. "I started bringing them home the day I made detective. I was photocopying pages and carrying them home in my bag before that." Emotion flickered in his eyes, and he peeled away from the wall, stepping closer, gaze fixed on her. "I go over them on the weekends or when I can't sleep. I keep thinking that one day something I've been missing will stand out."

Gwen moved, too, matching his stride, drawn to his goodness and strength. His compassion and perseverance. He'd done this for her. Gave up a future in architecture. Joined the force. Became a detective. And spent his free time in search of justice. For her.

The toes of their shoes bumped, and they stared at one another, a live wire of energy crackling between them.

She inhaled the warm, inviting scent of him, allowing it to envelope her. It would be so easy to reach for him. To stroke her hand up the length of his arm. To set a palm on his strong chest. To lean closer and fall into his embrace.

Lucas towered over her, his shoulders curving in and creating that nook where she'd always fit so perfectly. That place that had seemed carved just for her, where nothing bad could touch her. He lifted a hand slowly toward her cheek, watching carefully for signs the touch was unwanted. Another flinch, perhaps, like the one she'd accidentally given last night.

She wouldn't make that mistake again.

His phone buzzed, breaking the tension, and his hand fell back to his side. He retrieved the phone from his back pocket and pressed it to his ear without stepping away. "Winchester."

Gwen struggled to catch her breath, and her pulse beat between her ears.

His eyes caught hers once more, and he lowered the phone between them, giving the screen a tap with one thumb. "Gwen's here now, and you're on speaker. Go ahead."

"Miss Kind." Detective Anderson's voice rose from the phone. "We've had a chance to examine the full contents of the thumb drive recovered from your office. There were more than two thousand files."

Gwen's head lightened, and she stumbled back a step. How long had she been followed? How many photos had he taken of her each day? How had she not noticed?

"Two thousand?" Lucas repeated, anger coloring his tone. "How is that possible? Are we talking repeats? Like a photo shoot? Dozen or more photos of the same shot, from every session?"

"I'm afraid not," Detective Anderson said. "There were two thousand photos. Taken over the course of eight years."

Gwen's knees weakened, and her heart seized before breaking into a sprint. She was attacked six years ago.

"That's impossible," Lucas demanded, his tone defiant. "There must be some mistake."

"I'm sorry, but no," Detective Anderson answered. "Whoever left this thumb drive at Miss Kind's office last night has clearly been following her since two years before she was attacked. And leaving this behind suggests he wants her to know."

Chapter Nine

Lucas sat on the floor across from Gwen, take-out containers piled between them. He couldn't bring himself to leave her after the news Detective Anderson delivered, so he'd ordered her favorite takeout from a Chinese fusion restaurant they'd frequented in college. Then, he'd started sorting facts and photographs alongside her.

"Find anything?" she asked, a pot sticker captured between her chopsticks. She'd folded her legs into a pretzel and gone straight to work creating multiple piles from the photos Detective Anderson had sent him. Red curls hung over her shoulders, and there was deep concentration in her eyes.

"Nothing new," he said, shuffling through a mass of photos on his side of their makeshift picnic. All images of Gwen through the years. Some of the younger woman he'd known and loved. Others of this new Gwen, reborn and reinvented. On a jogging path. Outside her office. Lunching with friends. He'd yet to see a woman as beautiful as Gwen, and she still seemed completely unaware of that. He hated how much of her life he'd missed. "You?"

"Not really," she said, pushing a stack of images around with her free hand. "I'm trying desperately to look at this from someone else's perspective because when I let myself think about the fact that these are all photos of me, all taken by someone I didn't know was there, I want to move to Peoria." She bit into the pot sticker and chewed thoughtfully. "Maybe I could leave the country completely. I have some savings. Surely even this nut wouldn't follow me across the globe."

"If I thought moving would help, I'd help you pack myself," he said, "but you tried that once." He cast a pointed look at the photos around them. "I think we're going to have to see things through and catch this guy." He weighed his next words carefully. "Eight years is a long time."

She pressed her lips tight and set her chopsticks down. "More than a quarter of my life."

"It's a commitment. This guy is attached to you. He's bonded. In his mind, this is some kind of long-term relationship. And it's real."

Gwen wet her lips and averted her eyes. "I know."

Lucas felt a small sense of relief. It was important the victim understood the reality of the danger and situation fully. Gwen was smart and tough, but it was easy for anyone sitting at the eye of a storm not to see the full complexity of it. And that was paramount. "I've seen a lot of things since I started with the police force, but two thousand pictures over eight years? This is obsession, and it rarely ends well. My best guess is that something triggered him before, and something's set him off again. Whether that's something from his personal life or yours, I don't know." He trailed off, lifting then dropping a hand. He wasn't sure where or how to find this ghost, but if Gwen stayed with him, he could at least keep her safe while he tried.

"It's okay," she said. "I get it. It feels like we're starting over, but we're not. You've already done the research. We just have to reconsider everything you've collected with the new information in mind. Now we know he's a stalker first and foremost. A dedicated one, apparently." She huffed and rolled her eyes, then locked her gaze with his. "And I'm willing to fight this time. I ran before. As fast as I could, the moment the hospital discharged me. I did everything possible to avoid thinking about what I'd been through and what I'd lost. I'm not doing that again."

Lucas felt a fresh swell of pride at her determination. This woman was too much. And to be allowed into her new world, chosen as her partner in this? An honor.

"So." She picked up her chopsticks and forced a smile. "We can do this. Because we have to."

His lips twitched into a small smile. "I think I'm supposed to be the one giving the pep talks, but you're right. And that was pretty good."

"I'm pretty good at a lot of things," she said, blushing slightly as she lifted another bite to her mouth.

Lucas tried not to think about all the things she was good at. A few sordid images sprang to mind unbidden, and he shook his head to clear them. "Let's start from the beginning. What was your life like eight years ago?"

"Wow." She dug the fingers of one hand into her hair, pushing it behind her ear. "I've spent so long hyperfocused on the days immediately before my attack, I haven't given my freshman or sophomore year a single thought."

"At least we know when it started," he said. "You moved here from Florida for college, so this guy is someone you met at Bellemont or in town that year. What were your days like then? Your routines. Clubs or student organizations. Common hangouts?"

Gwen groaned. "Freshman year was tough. I was completely out of my element. I'd moved from a major city in Florida, where the ocean was everywhere I looked, to a small town in rural Kentucky where cows and cornfields outnumber cars and cabs. I stayed close to campus. Ate at the student center. Ran the campus track. I tried to show up and get involved with everything that happened on campus, sure that was how I'd find my groove and meet the friends I'd have for life." She sighed. "I was such a romantic. Everything was good in the world, and my future was full of endless possibilities."

"The world is good," Lucas said. Some people were absolute evil incarnate, sure, but the rest were good. "And your life is still full of endless possibilities."

Her lips parted, and hope flickered through the doubt in her eyes. "I suppose you think the best is yet to come and all that?"

"I'm certain of it," he said, willing her to believe him.

She returned her attention to the photos without comment or argument.

Lucas waited, watching as she considered the images before them. A chronicle of her adult life. From the lonely college freshman she'd described to the fierce twenty-seven-year-old with him today.

"There are a lot of photos from the hike-and-bike trail," she said. "Almost twice as many as those taken in other places this year. All the newest shots seem concentrated around my runs. It's where I first felt watched. The first time in years I realized someone was there."

Lucas finished his egg roll, then dusted his palms together. "Let's see."

She handed him a stack of photos. "I divided these into years, then again into locations. From there, I stacked them according to time. So, photos of me arriving at work are first. Going out to lunch are next, you get it. I wanted to see where and when he was most often. I thought we could check a calendar, too, see if he's only following me on certain days of the week. He can't work regular hours like me and most of the office employees I know, or he'd have to be at his office when I am. So, we know he's either unemployed, working part-time or on a flexible schedule."

Lucas marveled as he flipped through the stack she'd handed him. She was right. There were patterns. And the timeline of the photographer's availability was important. If matched to a suspect's work schedule, the timeline would be strong support for their case.

"How do you feel about another drive?" he asked, turning a photo in her direction. "We can go to the hike-and-bike trail. Try to find the place where he hid to take the photos based on the angles of the shots and landmarks captured in the images. Maybe he left a clue behind. Some kind of evidence, a nest or a blind."

"A nest?"

"A flattened area in the tall grass or excessive, centralized footprint among the trees. Maybe a clustering of trash, like wrappers from snacks or empty water bottles. Things that indicate someone spent a lot of time in that spot. If we're lucky, there'll be something we can use to track it back to one specific person." A jolt of adrenaline shot through him at the possibility.

Gwen leaned forward, a small smile creeping over her pretty face. "What are we waiting for?"

GWEN DIRECTED LUCAS to her preferred parking lot along the hike-and-bike trail. It was later in the day than she'd ever come, and the number of people was significantly higher. Still, the crowd here had nothing on the madhouse she'd jogged more recently.

Lucas swung his pickup into an empty spot and settled the engine, taking his time to observe the scene before climbing out.

She scanned the familiar area, hating the fear that pebbled her skin. She'd started most of her days here for years. It was beautiful, always clean and well-maintained with benches and signs identifying indigenous flora and fauna every quarter mile or so for breaks and education. The parking lot was conveniently located at the end of a short winding road, easily accessed from a much busier one. A camp of trees separated the trail from the main road; the trail went on for miles, paralleling a set of old railroad tracks.

"Ready?" Lucas turned to her inside the warm cab, patient and assessing, as always.

If she said no, he'd start the truck and leave. No questions. No judgment or pressure. That was who Lucas was, but she had to stop running. So, she nodded. Unable to speak around a sudden knot in her throat and burst of nerves in her gut.

She'd promised herself she'd never go back on the trail, but she'd also asked Lucas for his help, then demanded he let her be involved. Now it was time to trust him to protect her, and get out of his way so he could work.

They climbed out and met at the truck's front bumper.

A couple on bikes pedaled past, and a man walking a dog stepped aside to give them space.

Lucas moved onto the trail behind the bikes, walking the dense tree line. "Do the trees grow along both sides of the trail like this for a long distance?" he asked, peering in each direction.

"Yes." She crossed her arms and hurried to catch up, feeling watched, even now. The trees she'd once loved for their beauty and solitude were actually the perfect hiding spot for a psychopath and his camera, she realized. Her stomach rocked with the thought.

"No good," Lucas muttered, waving from one side of the path to the other. "An attacker could drag a victim out of sight in seconds here."

Gwen shivered, wrapping her arms more tightly around her.

"I don't see any signs of a security patrol or cameras," Lucas said, squinting up at the telephone poles. "The hike-and-bike trail is maintained by local park services. Did you ever see park security or any other kind of patrol out here?"

"No." And how stupid was it that she'd continually come here believing she was alone?

She'd thought the danger was behind her. That she was a woman who'd been in the wrong place at the wrong time and suffered the consequences. Not the victim of a stalker.

She'd been concentrating on emotional healing and learning to let go of the trauma. All the while, she'd been putting herself in harm's way and thinking it was the right thing to do.

She groaned inwardly at all the times she'd gotten spooked and had forced herself to keep her chin up and finish her jog. She'd even congratulated herself on the days she'd persevered. Chanting internally that there was nothing to be afraid of.

Lucas whistled and slipped into the trees several yards ahead. "I think we've got something," he said. "Do you have the photos?"

Gwen hurried to meet him. She sorted through the photos, finding landmarks to orient herself. The telephone pole. A section of wooden fence. "Here." She passed the stack to Lucas. "This is the right place."

Lucas moved deeper into the trees, then bumped the toe of his shoe against the ground. A patch of earth was rubbed free of grass and littered in tiny debris. Gum foils and candy wrappers. Empty water bottles that had been smashed and tucked into the rotting stump of a tree. "I think this is it." He pulled a phone from his pocket and dialed. "You're dedicated to your routines, so he probably started coming early and waiting for you. Traffic noise this close to the road and parking lot would've masked his sounds."

He continued to toe the ground until his shoe caught on a string. "This is Detective Lucas Winchester for Detective Anderson," he said into the phone, then squatted to pull on the string.

Slowly, the red nylon rope came through the strategically arranged pile of leaves. Thicker than she'd originally thought, the durable outdoor line ran a dozen feet deeper into the woods. Lucas knocked away a heap of sticks and removed a small camouflaged bag. He tugged a set of Nitrile gloves from his coat pocket and slid them over his hands while relaying the situation to whoever listened on the other end of his call.

Gwen gripped the trunk of a tree for stability as she watched, openmouthed.

Lucas worked the drawstring on the bag and upturned it, dumping the contents onto a swath of dirt. A full bottle of water fell out, then a mass of freezer bags, each filled with a different snack or supply. Bandages. Over-the-counter painkillers. Beef jerky. Granola and nuts. Lucas gripped the bag with both hands and gave it another shake.

A large, oddly shaped item fell onto the pile. Its appearance elicited an immediate curse from Lucas while Gwen's mind struggled to understand.

He lifted the item carefully, pressing the phone to his shoulder with his ear and scowling deeply. "And an eight-inch hunting knife." He pulled the stiff sheath away, leaving a shiny silver blade in his opposite hand.

Gwen struggled for breath as images of her attack flashed through her mind. The scar along her side burned as she recalled the feeling of it plunged into her flesh. Desperation clawed at her throat and chest as she fell through time, suddenly present in the moments that had changed everything.

Lucas marched back onto the trail, indignant, describing their location to Detective Anderson while Gwen worked to stay conscious.

The psycho had packed a bag of snacks to pass the time while he watched her run.

And a massive knife to kill her.

She leaned forward at the waist and braced her palms against her knees, feeling the familiar wave of tension and fear take over. She pressed her eyelids shut, pulling herself into the present and forcing away the awful images. "Keep it together, Gwen," she whispered to herself.

Branches rumbled overhead as a mass of birds lifted from the treetops.

And a hand clamped hard across her mouth.

Another arm snaked around her center and hauled her back into the trees. The sharp point of a knife pressed strategically against her throat.

Chapter Ten

Lucas moved in long strides through the woods toward the hike-and-bike trail, trying to improve the cell signal and locate the nearest post with a mile marker to pinpoint their location. "We're at mile eighteen," he told Detective Anderson. "Send a crime scene team in an unmarked car. We want to get the job done without the fanfare of a lights and sirens parade. Especially if he's watching. Even if he's not, Gwen's struggling. I want to get her out of here as soon as possible."

The hair on Lucas's arms rose with a change in the air as he pivoted back in the direction he'd come. The trees rattled with a sudden mass exodus of birds, and his gut clenched.

His feet were in motion before he'd made the conscious effort to run. "Gwen?" he called, hoping his instincts were wrong, praying his nerves were just frayed. That she was safe where he'd left her, only a few yards away. "Gwen!"

"What's happening?" Detective Anderson demanded, her voice exploding from the phone he'd nearly forgotten he was holding.

He burst back through the trees and spotted Gwen immediately. A man in a ghillie suit stood behind her, one hand covering her mouth, the opposite arm snaked around her middle, just below her ribs, a large hunting knife in his fist. The fabric of his camouflage blended seamlessly with the surroundings, and Lucas couldn't help wondering just how close the man had been when Lucas had run off, distracted by a need to report his findings. How close had the attacker been when Lucas left her alone and in danger?

"Stop!" Lucas screamed, storming forward as he pressed the phone more tightly to his ear. "He's here. He's got her. I need backup. Now!" He plunged the phone into his jacket pocket, then unholstered his sidearm.

They were moving toward the road on the other side of the trees.

Gwen's eyes were wide with terror as the assailant dragged her backward. Her hands clutched at his arms, and she winced each time they stumbled over fallen saplings and branches.

A spot of blood spread through her jacket below the blade now glinting in the afternoon sunlight. The same blade that Lucas had just dumped from the bag and left on the forest floor to be used against her.

"Take another step, and I will shoot you," he promised, advancing steadily on the much slower pair. "I won't let you hurt her again."

The assailant looked over his shoulder, his face covered with layers of fringed camouflaged material and a thin black balaclava, revealing only his crazed eyes. The elaborate suit made him seem more like a ghost than a man. He was taller than Gwen by several inches, though hunched; it was difficult to guess with any precision. His shoulders were broader, arms and legs longer, and the boots he wore left an occasional imprint deep in the ground.

Lucas grinned. The man was armed, but he was no match for Lucas's marksmanship. All he needed was one clear shot.

Traffic sounds grew louder with each step, the busy road beyond the dense patch of forest drawing nearer.

"Stop!" Lucas called again, mind reeling, assessing, troubleshooting. Did this guy have a plan beyond snatch-and-grab? Did he leave a getaway car nearby? Parked along the winding road into the little lot, perhaps? Or parked along the busy street? Ready to help them vanish.

Lucas lengthened his strides, pushing forward, refusing to lose her again. "You're running out of forest," he warned, letting a sneer work over his deceptively cool face.

"Stay back," the would-be abductor called, his voice unnaturally low.

Disguised, Lucas realized.

"Stop moving or I'll gut her," he seethed, dragging the blade into position beneath her sternum.

Lucas's steps stuttered, and bile rose in his throat.

Gwen's eyes fluttered shut as they breached the

wooded area and stepped into the blinding afternoon sunlight along the road.

Her attacker moved the knife again, seeking better purchase on her frame and turning them away from the streaming cars. The layers of the ghillie suit lifted and fluttered on the breeze. "Stay back!" he screamed, voice frantic as he looked in every direction. Exposed to a hundred commuters, some who were now slowing at the sight of him holding a captive at knifepoint. He whipped his face in the direction of distant sirens rising into the sky.

Gwen's eyes opened and locked with Lucas's once more.

"You can't get away this time," Lucas warned, stepping slowly forward and lining up a shot for the next time the assailant turned away. "Might as well let her go and take that suit off so we can see who we're dealing with."

The man shifted, releasing his grip on Gwen so quickly, Lucas barely perceived it before she was flying away from the man. Shoved hard. Into traffic.

The scream that ripped from her core nearly split Lucas in two. The blare of a horn pushed his heart into his throat.

The assailant broke right, sprinting back into the woods as Gwen crashed onto the asphalt and bounced slightly before becoming still.

Tires screeched, and Lucas launched himself after her. Cars careened out of their way, thankfully already somewhat slowed by the public abduction attempt. The sounds of multiple low speed collisions rocketed around them, spewing chunks of headlights and dropping portions of fenders, as one car clipped another vehicle, then another, only feet away from Gwen's prone body.

Lucas wrenched her off the ground, waving an arm at oncoming cars as she groaned and jerked to life. "Shh!" he soothed, guiding her back to the berm of grass outside the tree line.

Her legs fumbled to keep pace, and her hands gripped the material of his coat.

The scent of burning rubber from squealing tires mixed with angry voices and sirens in the air.

Her assailant was gone. Vanished back into the trees. But Lucas couldn't leave Gwen. He wouldn't let her bleed and suffer alone, not ever again.

She sobbed against his chest, fingers fiercely knotted into the fabric of his coat as emergency vehicles lined the busy road. "He came from the trees," she said, heartbroken. "He was there all along. Waiting."

Lucas gathered her closer, horrified by the afternoon's events and reverent for the outcome. "We'll find him. I promise. You're okay now. The ambulance is here."

An unmarked sedan took the turn toward the parking lot. Likely the low-key crime scene crew he'd requested. Followed by a set of cruisers, lights flashing, and a line of ambulances, probably dispatched for the fender benders. He swallowed a humorless chuckle at the irony.

He tugged Gwen back for a look at her side, the ambulances reminding him this wasn't over. She could still be seriously hurt. "How bad is the cut? Did you break anything when you fell?"

"I'm okay." She loosened her grip on him and stepped away slightly, forcing him to release her in turn. Far sooner than he was ready.

"You're really not okay," he said gently. "That's the shock talking. You're going to need to get checked out, and probably stitches." He turned to wave an arriving ambulance closer, and it wedged itself onto the berm at their side.

The passenger door flew open and a familiar man jumped down. "Lucas!" The paramedic raced to them, a look of confusion on his youthful face. "What are you doing here?"

"Is that Isaac?" Gwen whispered, eyes wide at the sight of him.

Lucas smiled at his younger cousin and close friend. "The one and only."

"What happened?" Isaac asked, still taking in the scene.

Isaac was the youngest of the Winchesters, though a cousin by blood, he'd practically been raised in Lucas's family home, making Isaac the unofficial little brother in most of their childhood memories. A brother he didn't see often enough these days.

Isaac reached gingerly for Gwen as he waited for Lucas to explain. His gaze ran quickly over her, assessing the work ahead of him. When his eyes met hers, he froze. "Gwen?"

She nodded, rubbing shaky hands across her face.

"Hi, Isaac." She winced and pressed both palms against her side.

His gaze followed to the growing blood spot on her jacket, then snapped back to Lucas. "Pick her up, let's get her into the bus. What the hell happened out here today?"

Lucas pulled one of Gwen's arms over his shoulders, then bent to sweep her off her feet before she could protest. He cradled her body to his as he jogged the short distance to the ambulance. "We think her attacker is back, and he got a hold of her today."

Isaac blanched. "You're going to be okay," he told her, his jaw setting with resolve. "How are you feeling?" He opened the bay doors and stood aside while Lucas carried her to the gurney inside. "Cold? Dizzy? Nauseous?"

"A little," she answered, her teeth beginning to chatter.

Isaac covered her with a white blanket, then fixed a stethoscope into his ears. Her tragedy had changed him, too.

Gwen set a palm against his cheek as he worked, listening to her heart and lungs. "Look at you." She sniffled, and a tear swiveled over her cheek. "You're all grown up. I'm sorry I missed it."

"Me, too," he said, checking her vitals before pulling a bag of IV fluids from a cabinet behind him. He hung the bag, then worked the line into her hand, smoothly inserting the needle without her seeming to notice. Satisfied, he turned cautious eyes back on hers. "I'm glad to see you again, too, but we could've just had lunch."

Gwen smiled, then winced once more.

Isaac pulled back with a patient grin. "I need to take a look at that." He cut the material of her shirt, exposing the wound in Gwen's side, then deftly cleaned and assessed. "You'll need a couple stitches, but this will heal. It's not deep." He applied a topical cream and bandage with skilled and confident hands. "We'll get the sutures at the hospital, and better evaluate that bump on your head."

Her hand rose to her forehead. She grimaced as her fingers found the rising knot.

"She hit her head on the road when he shoved her into traffic," Lucas said.

Isaac swore under his breath, then moved on to cleaning superficial wounds. First her palms, then cutting away the torn fabric of her pants to work on her knees. "He's really back?" he asked. "After all this time?" He looked up from his work, catching Lucas's eye.

"Turns out, he never left," Gwen said.

Isaac's gaze hardened. A silent order for Lucas to find this guy and put him away. As if that wasn't Lucas's new purpose in life.

"When did you decide to be a paramedic?" Gwen asked. "I thought you were going to study computer science."

"I decided I wanted to make a difference," he said, smoothing a bandage over the broken skin of her palm.

Isaac had spent every minute he was allowed in the

hospital hallways and waiting rooms while Gwen had fought for her life. Then became a dedicated visitor during her recovery. He'd been crushed to learn she'd left for Florida without saying goodbye. Gwen had been his family, too. When he'd changed his choice of major freshman year of college, he'd told his mother there weren't any computer technicians involved in saving Gwen, but there had been countless medical professionals. He wanted to be like them.

"Hey!" A man in a local PD jacket waved a badge overhead, scowling and summoning Lucas from outside the open ambulance doors.

Isaac and the driver looked to Lucas.

"Are we okay here for another minute?" Lucas asked. "I'd like to talk to this guy, but I want to go with Gwen to the hospital."

Gwen reached for his hand. "Go. I'm okay here, and I want to know what he says."

"I'll be right back." Lucas hopped down to meet the man with the badge, hopeful the assailant had fallen on his own knife while running away.

"Lucas Winchester?" he asked.

"Yes, sir." Lucas extended a hand to the older officer. "West Liberty, SVU."

"Is our vic going to be okay?" The officer tipped his chin to the waiting ambulance. Sincere concern lined his brow.

"That's Gwen Kind," Lucas reported. "She's not a victim, and she's going to be just fine."

The officer seemed to consider that a moment as he

watched Gwen on the gurney, then nodded. "Good. Detective Anderson wants to talk with you. She said not to let you leave until she did."

"I'm in a hurry," Lucas said, unwilling to be detained longer than necessary. "She can catch me at the local ER. Any news on the assailant?"

A sharp whistle drew their attention to the tree line. "I'll take it from here," Anderson reported, stepping onto the shoulder and taking in the scene.

An ambulance on the berm. A closed lane of traffic, courtesy of several crunched cars. A set of uniformed officers and an arriving tow truck, attempting to clear it all.

She excused the officer before Lucas with the flick of her head, then gave Lucas a cold stare. "What exactly were you doing out here? Investigating a crime in my jurisdiction?" she huffed the questions, cheeks pink with temper. "You only called to tell me what you were up to after the fact. Then by happenstance, I got to hear about that poor woman being abducted while you chased her and her assailant into traffic. Now, I have an injured woman, a crime scene, a pile of wrecked cars and a stalker who's both on the run and onto us. How the hell did he even find you here? Tell me a detective with a record as good as yours isn't being followed without knowing."

Lucas blinked. How *had* he found them there? In the middle of the day. Not at all according to Gwen's routine? What had she said when Lucas pulled her out of traffic? He'd come from the trees?

"If I had any chance of finding this guy before he knew I was looking," Anderson ranted on, "it went straight out the window the moment you decided to take on a New Plymouth case without any authority to do so. Do you understand what a loss that is? A disadvantage you gave me."

She worked her jaw and crossed her arms, turning her back to the ambulance. "I understand on a human level what you're doing here with her and why. I've read more about Ms. Kind's original attack over the past few days than I have ever read about any other cold case. Ever. And I get what this means to you, but this is my town, and I lead the investigations here. Whatever personal connection you have with the victim might be solid motivation for you, but it isn't doing you or your friend any favors. So, I suggest you take a big boy step back or the next time you cause chaos like this, I'll contact your supervisor and have you sent home."

Lucas narrowed his eyes, hating every word she'd said and the tone in which the message had been delivered. "With all due respect," he began, ready to explain a few things that weren't respectful at all, but he froze. Another thought pressed its way into mind, stunning him temporarily silent.

"Yes?" Detective Anderson demanded. "You've got something to say?"

"We came here today after reviewing the photo files you sent me. Did you include every photo from the thumb drive?"

She nodded, brows furrowed. "Everything. Why?"

Lucas shoved his hands through his hair and gritted his teeth. "We're here because there were twice as many photos of this place than any other location in the past year. It was the most obvious place to start looking for clues, so we came." He groaned and swallowed a thick line of curses. He'd been tricked. Manipulated. Beaten. "This guy knew we'd make that connection and come here to investigate. He set us up. He hid. And he waited."

Hunted, Lucas realized. They'd been lured like deer by poachers. "And he even left himself a knife for when we inevitably came waltzing into his trap."

Chapter Eleven

Gwen climbed into the bed in Lucas's room just after nine. They'd been trapped at the hospital in New Plymouth for hours, waiting for her to receive medical attention, then for the staff to observe and discharge her. They'd made their statements to the local police department, telling the story at length, and on repeat, to be sure nothing was missed or forgotten. Then Detective Anderson had laid into Lucas for inserting himself into her investigation and causing the pile of fender benders among other things. Gwen had done her best to settle the woman's temper, but she was beside herself, and Gwen hadn't had the energy to argue. She'd just wanted to go home.

"You don't have to do all this," she told Lucas for the dozenth time as he worked on stoking the fire.

"Temperatures are dropping tonight," he reminded her, shooting a sheepish look over his shoulder. "You'll be glad I did. The furnace in this place hasn't been updated since we were in middle school. Having a fireplace in the bedroom is practically a necessity."

"You've fussed too much already. It's been an awful

day. Let's just call it and start again tomorrow." She rubbed her stinging eyes and yawned, pushed closer to sleep by the day's excitement and whatever had been in her IV, no doubt.

He stretched onto his feet, dusting his palms and surveying the room. He'd gathered his discarded clothing and closed the closet door while she'd showered and changed into pajamas. When she'd returned, the space was spotless, and there was a glass of water on the nightstand beside the prescribed pain medication she refused to take and the bottle of over-the-counter stuff she'd reluctantly said she might. The prescription would make her head foggy. She couldn't afford that now. The aspirin was a better option, once the medication from the hospital wore off.

He'd insisted they stay here tonight, when she'd wanted to go to her place, but that was a fight she'd be better equipped for tomorrow. For now, they were safe in his home. Back in his jurisdiction, where Detective Anderson couldn't complain about their investigation, which was nice. And hopefully, Gwen's attacker would be lying low tonight, recovering from his failure and allowing Gwen and Lucas to rest.

She tracked him with a tired, apologetic gaze as he crossed back to her. She'd come to him for an opinion and advice, now he'd inadvertently become her personal protector and caretaker.

"Hey," he said softly, sinking onto the bed at her side. His baggy sweatshirt and pants made him look younger and softer, like the man she'd fallen in love with in college. His hair was mussed from dragging his fingers through it and damp from a shower. His scent so familiar and enticing, she wanted to pull him against her and thank him properly for saving her life today.

More effects of that pesky IV, she assured herself.

She was too relaxed, and it was hard to corral her thoughts. Her mind circled around how good it felt to be with Lucas again, whatever else happened. How she felt more whole here, with a man she hadn't seen or spoken to in years, than she had any day in between. And her heart grew heavy, hating how hard it would be to leave again, and how empty her days would become without him. She couldn't stay with Lucas, and he couldn't come with her once this ended. They each had their own lives now, and no amount of wistful, IV-induced hope could change that.

"Tired?" he asked, a small grin on his handsome face. He caressed her forehead and cheeks before taking her hand.

Her restless heart leapt, and it took another long beat for her to realize he was checking her temperature and pulse.

She scooted up in bed, arranging the pillows behind her as a backrest. "I'm okay," she promised, then cringed slightly at the spear of pain along her newly sutured side. "Thank you for everything you're doing. And for saving my life."

Lucas's caring eyes searched hers. "There's an argument to be made that I'm the one who put you in danger by taking you with me today, and by not seeing his trap for what it was."

"Ridiculous," Gwen said, pushing herself up straighter

against the pillows. "You're stuck in the middle of this because of me, and we went to the park together. As a team," she said. "I'm not here to hide out while you fix my problems. I'm here because I needed to know if you thought there was something to worry about. There clearly is, and you're helping me through it. Which is incredibly kind and gracious of you." Not to mention heroic, gallant and a dozen other wonderful things. "There was no way you could have predicted he'd be there today."

"Because I underestimated him," Lucas said. His cool blue eyes turning away, brooding again. Something he'd been making a profession out of since they'd ridden away from the crime scene in the ambulance. And it broke her heart.

"This isn't on you," she whispered, wondering where he went when he drifted away in one of those remorseful stares. A painful possibility occurred as she watched him draw into himself and noted the guilt and shame in his eyes. The way he was all-in with her from the moment someone had picked up their tab at the pub, and the way he mothered her now, trying to make every detail right. As if fresh bedding and the perfect fire would somehow heal her faster. Or make amends. "Luke," she whispered, forcing the word from her lips. "Do you blame yourself for what happened to me in college?"

His attention snapped back to her, a world of pain and hurt coursing behind hooded eyes. "Every day."

Her breath caught and her throat tightened. Unsure what to say, she reached for him, dragging him nearer by the sleeve of his shirt. He resisted a moment, confusion clouding his gaze. Then, he followed her lead and allowed her to hold him. A sea of emotions broke over her as she pressed him closer. It had been years since she'd touched or been touched by anyone other than her parents. And that had been polite and limited. She'd feared that being touched could send her into a spiral of memories she didn't want. Memories of the monster and all the ways he'd hurt her. But now, as Lucas belatedly wrapped his arms around her, the opposite was happening. It was as if she could finally breathe.

Her head fell easily into the crook of his neck, and she loved the feel of his heart beating against hers. "It's not your fault," she said. "Not what happened today and not what happened before. I promise you." He shuddered against her, and for a moment she wondered if he was crying. She wouldn't blame him if he was. Hers was the same message he'd repeated to her all those years ago, begging her to see her attack wasn't about some wrong choice she'd made, but about the attacker alone. She wasn't responsible for anyone else's behavior, and she had every right to walk home that night, or any night. No reason to think that choice would change her life. She couldn't shoulder any of that burden any longer, and neither should Lucas.

"I'm sorry I left you," she said gently, the truth flowing from her heart and through her lips without filter. The moment was too precious to ruin with veils and lies. Something had changed for her today, and she knew instinctually that this was the moment all the others had been leading to since that night. It was time to set Lucas free from any of the weight she'd unintentionally left on him when she'd walked away. "I ran away for a thousand really good reasons, but I should have handled our goodbye better."

Lucas pulled back, eyes tight with emotion. "You did what you needed to do. I never blamed or judged you for that. Not for a minute."

A smile tugged Gwen's trembling lips. "I was wrong, and I'm sorry. I loved you, and I owed you a proper goodbye."

His frown deepened. "Gwen, you've never owed me anything."

"I do." She worked to press back the painful lump in her throat. There was one more thing that needed to be said before she changed her mind. "I let a monster change me, but I didn't mean to let him change you, too."

Lucas shook his head slowly. "He didn't change me."

"No? So, you like being a Special Victims Unit detective?" she asked. "Dealing with this kind of brutality and horror every day. A constant reminder of what you went through?"

He turned stormy eyes on her without answering.

"You were going to be a great architect," she said, grieving the future he'd lost. "You had more brains and talent than anyone else in your class. And you gave that up. I think joining the force was noble, but this was never your dream."

"You were my dream," he said flatly. "You."

"But I was gone. And you quit school."

Lucas ground his teeth, eyes flooded with barely contained emotion. Anger, heartbreak and regret among others she couldn't name. "I didn't need my master's degree to join the force."

"You were never supposed to join the force."

"And I didn't quit school, I flunked out."

"What?" She pulled her chin back, stunned. "How?"

"I might've been a grad student at Bellemont, but I spent all my time looking for the man who hurt you. I looked for clues on my own, interviewing students and tracking leads. I blanketed the campus with flyers in search of anything that could further the case. My grades were in the trash by the end of the first semester. That was when I realized I didn't want to be an architect anymore. And what I really needed to find the man who hurt you was access to everything the police knew so far. There was only one way to do that. So, I joined the force. Not that it's gotten me any closer to my goal."

"Are you happy?" she asked. "As a detective?" That was the bottom line, she supposed. Even if she couldn't understand finding joy in being surrounded by people living her nightmare, if Lucas somehow could, then that was all that mattered.

"Yeah," he answered easily, and with a small laugh. "I am." He turned those intense blue eyes on her with a smile. "I like making a difference. I like seeing criminals punished, and I like seeing victims get the justice they deserve. When I get to be part of that delivery, all the better. I might've come to law enforcement by way of the unthinkable, but I've stayed for me. For them." He shrugged. "Sitting where I am today, I'm not sure I'd be happy as an architect. So, no, that psychopath didn't change me, but he will regret he ever crossed me."

The words hit her like a punch to the chest. If Lucas hadn't changed, then she'd never really known him. He wasn't an alpha-male, gun-wielding lawman. He was a peacekeeper who loved numbers and old buildings. Wasn't he?

"What?" he asked. "Tell me what you're thinking. You look unhappy, and I don't know why. Was it something I said?"

"No. Not at all. I'm glad you're happy, and that you're being honest. I guess I'm just wondering how well I ever knew you." She glanced away, around the beautiful old room in a historic house he was renovating on a cop's salary and in his spare time. "You still love architecture."

"I still love a lot of things." He shifted on the bed to face her. "I'm the same man I've always been. I changed career paths, that's all, and our careers don't define us."

"Then why aren't you married?" she asked, cheeks heating with fatigue and frustration at her unintentional candor. "You date, but you haven't settled down. That's a big change from what I thought I knew. I always thought you wanted a wife and family. Carpool and Little League."

"I still do, and I don't date," he said, brows furrowed in confusion. "Why'd you say that?"

She frowned back at him, sorry to have pressed into his personal business, and certain she'd hate whatever he said next. "I heard the guys at the station talking while I was waiting to see you. They said you had flavors of the week." She huffed a sigh. "Don't answer that. It doesn't matter, and those guys weren't talking to me.

I'm just cranky and tired. I should sleep." She punched the pillow at her side, leaning slightly forward with a wince to adjust them before she lay back.

Lucas pushed onto his feet, giving her room for the silent tantrum. "I lie to the guys about my dating life so I can be alone," he said. "I don't want to hang out with them after work because I have a ton to do here. I don't want to argue with them or offend them, so I tell them I have dates."

"But you don't?"

"Not in a long time, and it never felt quite right when I did." He gripped the back of his neck as he walked toward the door. "Truth is that there was only ever one woman for me. If I couldn't be with her, then what was the point?" He paused in the doorway. "I hope you're able to get some rest." He flipped out the light and walked away.

LUCAS HEADED FOR his home office. He needed to check in at work. As suspected, Detective Anderson had already spoken with his superior, so Lucas had the pleasure of rehashing the awful day one more time. Thankfully, protocols aside, his supervisor had his back.

He disconnected the call feeling only slightly better than he had before making it. His neck and shoulder muscles were pinched and achy, his limbs and mind heavy with fatigue. Lucas was drained. Emotionally, physically and mentally. He needed a decent night's sleep and a fresh start tomorrow, when his head was clear and he wasn't saying whatever came to mind. He cringed internally at the memory of telling Gwen he didn't date, and that she was the only woman he'd ever wanted.

He listened to a long line of voice mail updates on his current caseload, then forced himself through some paperwork online. He didn't hear from Gwen again, and by the time the clock struck midnight, he was ready to call it a night.

Lucas locked the house down before setting his alarm and checking in on Gwen once more. She looked peaceful and perfect cuddled under his comforter, warmed by his fire. Maybe it was the influence of exhaustion on his clarity or the emotional impact of seeing her in a madman's clutches, but Lucas was certain losing her again, when this was over, would be more than his heart could bear.

Chapter Twelve

Gwen woke with a headache, likely from the goose egg on her forehead, dehydration and the knowledge that she'd said some overly revealing things to Lucas the night before. She scooted upright and winced at the pain in her side. Memories of the previous day's near-abduction raced back, images from the nightmare that had kept her stirring through the night.

She took inventory of her many aches and pains, then downed a pair of aspirins along with the glass of water on the nightstand. The house was silent outside her room, and she panicked, momentarily, afraid Lucas had left her alone. She pulled the covers higher under her arms, then dialed Lucas, hoping that if he had gone, he would be back soon.

The ring of her call echoed through the receiver of her phone, as well as in the hall outside her door.

Lucas appeared a moment later, wide awake and dressed for the day. His faded jeans hung low on his hips. A worn gray T-shirt peeked from beneath an un-buttoned flannel. The blue plaid pattern emphasized his brilliant eyes and the way he'd rolled the sleeves to his elbows highlighted the ropes of muscle along his forearm.

Gwen disconnected and forced her mouth shut.

"You're up?" he asked, rhetorically, slipping his cell phone into his jeans pocket. "How did you sleep?"

"Okay," she said. "All things considered."

"Restless?" he guessed, leaning against the jamb. The shift in position opened the flannel further, revealing the way his T-shirt stretched to accommodate his broad chest.

"Yeah. You?"

He shrugged, then crossed his arms. "How's your side? And your head? Are you in pain?"

"I've been through worse," she said wryly, hating how much that was true. "I've been thinking."

"Uh oh."

"Funny." She narrowed her eyes. "Do you need to go in to work today, or do you have time for a field trip? Something local this time, so Detective Anderson can't complain."

Lucas cocked his head and watched her carefully before nodding. "I talked to my sergeant last night. Filled him in on what's happening, and he assigned me to your case. It's officially reopened, and I can work in the field, checking in periodically."

Gwen's heart skipped, both at the idea of spending more uninterrupted time with Lucas, and at the idea her case was reopened. It had been closed when they'd had nothing more to go on. Opening the case meant there was new hope. Something she'd been without for far too long. "So, you're in for the field trip?"

He nodded.

"You didn't ask what I have in mind." She frowned. "I've been laying here for the last hour going over all your possible complaints and making watertight arguments against them."

Lucas let his arms fall to his sides, and a grin tugged lazily at his lips. "We can argue first, if you want, but since you're going to win anyway, I guess I'll just do what you say."

Her smile widened. "A lady could get used to that."

Ninety minutes later, Gwen climbed down from the cab of Lucas's truck and surveyed the college campus she'd once loved dearly. The aspirin, combined with a generous amount of water at breakfast, had taken the edge off, and she was ready to start at the beginning. At Bellemont.

"Ready?" he asked, eyes narrowed in scrutiny. Clearly, Lucas had reservations about her idea to retrace her freshman and sophomore year tracks, or as many tracks as she could remember anyway. It seemed logical that being back on campus would help her recall her early routines.

"Ready." She forced her shoulders back, certain he could see through her thinly veiled bravado, but determined to be strong. "We should head for the student center. My dorm was down that way, along with most of my classes. And we'll pass the computer lab on the way. We can make a loop, concentrate on the places I frequented. And visit the crime scene before we go."

"I don't think that's necessary," Lucas protested.

"It is," she assured him, then with a hard internal shove, she forced her feet to move.

Lucas fell into step at her side, tense and overly concerned, his two most common moods these days. He'd tugged on a knit beanie and pulled a black motorcycle jacket over his flannel. Between the ensemble and the scowl, he looked more like trouble than the law.

She'd settled for a jean jacket over her favorite cream turtleneck layered with a comfy tank top, jeans and brown leather boots. Her cream mittens and hat were speckled with gold, and her wild red curls lifted like a halo around her face with each fresh gust of wind.

They walked silently through the brisk day, past multiple parking lots, through common areas with meandering students, and around a group of prospective freshmen receiving a campus tour.

Sounds of the school's marching band rose into the day, punctuated by a cheering crowd and the mumbling of an emcee over the stadium speakers.

"Sounds like a pep rally," Lucas said, staring into the distance as the fight song blared.

Scents of hot dogs and popcorn peppered the air beside the ashy aroma of a bonfire. Was it even fall in Kentucky if no one had a bonfire?

"Spirit week," Gwen said. "I used to love these days." There was something about the camaraderie they provoked. The staff and student body came together with alumni to celebrate everything Bellemont. People were happy. The air was electric with anticipation of all that was to come.

Today was no different, and the nostalgia was palpable. It took immense self-control not to reach for Lucas's hand as they walked the familiar paths.

"Still doing okay?" he asked, slowing his pace when fear came bubbling back in her.

"Yeah." She nodded, then pushed her feet forward once more, refocused on the memories she needed, and forcing out those she didn't. "Let's make the library and computer lab a priority today, then the student center. I had most of my meals there freshman and sophomore year."

She rolled her shoulders back and forced her chin up. It was her idea to be here, and Lucas was letting her lead the charge. The least she could do was try not to look as apprehensive as she felt. She'd managed to lever her reluctant self from the truck, and get this far. There was no turning back now. It was time to explore and remember.

Lucas cleared his throat as they turned up the next path. "I was thinking about the fact that you were being followed for two years before we knew it." He shot a sideways look in her direction, then forced his hands into his pockets. "Then you were attacked on the weekend of our engagement. The night you went out with friends to celebrate."

Her steps faltered, and flashes of the attack rushed back to her. Angry hands in her hair. Cold eyes behind a black balaclava. A blow to her chest. Searing pain in her side.

"Hey," a man's voice called.

Gwen snapped back to the present, a sheen of sweat on her temple and brow.

The man nodded as he approached, pumping a fist in the air.

Lucas lifted a fist in reciprocation as they passed on the wide stone path.

Gwen angled to watch the group as they disappeared into the crowd behind them. "Who was that?"

"I have no idea," Lucas said with a laugh. "Other alumni, I'd guess."

She chuckled with him. That sounded right. "We're all friends now. At least for another two or three days."

There were people everywhere, plenty who were unfamiliar and others who weren't. Gwen had already spotted a former teacher and one or two classmates in the crowd. Everyone looked the same, if a little heavier and most with shorter hair.

Hope mixed with dread in her gut at the thought of seeing any of her friends while she was at Bellemont. She didn't want their pitying looks or to entertain polite but meaningless conversation. Gwen was on a mission. "Computer lab," she said, pointing to the next building on their right.

Lucas held the door for her as she slipped inside. The scent of burnt coffee assaulted her senses as she climbed the steps to the second floor. Balloon bouquets stood cheerfully outside key rooms, set up for guests and visitors.

She tugged off her mittens and stowed them in her pockets as they made their way down the hall.

The computer lab door had a "Welcome" sign.

Gwen peeked around the corner before taking a tentative step across the threshold. An empty room spread out before them, and a ripple of memories rushed through her. Same tables and chairs. Same whiteboards and motivational posters. She trailed her fingertips across the cool surfaces, feeling an unexpected smile grow. "I spent so much time here those first two years. I didn't understand the engineering software at all, among other things, and I still have a love-hate relationship with databases." She gave a soft laugh.

Lucas stopped at the large desk up front and surveyed the scene. Someone had decorated the whiteboard in school colors and made a pom-pom-and-confetti boarder with dry erase markers. A pile of flyers with the week's itinerary stood neatly at the corner of the teacher's desk. Lucas pressed a palm to the nearby mug. "Still warm. We must've just missed whoever was here. Do you want to wait?"

"No." Gwen completed her circle through the room, feeling lighter than she had since she'd first stepped onto campus. "We can come back."

He swung an arm wide, and she met him at the doorway.

Her long-guarded heart began to beat harder as he set a palm against her back. Being there with Lucas, old memories colliding with new ones and the tender way he still looked at her was almost too much. And she wondered again what life would have been like if she hadn't run away. If she'd come back to him instead of setting up some facsimile of a life, alone, in the next town. She'd fallen asleep thinking of the way he'd said his dreams never changed, and that there was only ever one woman for him.

If that was all true, when this was finally over, was there a chance he'd ask her to stay? Could he still want her, broken pieces and all? Was it fair to hope he would?

Lucas kept one eye on Gwen as they moved through knots and clusters of people along the walkways outside. She'd done well so far. Put on a brave face at first, then seemed genuinely at ease in more familiar spaces.

The path curved and forked ahead of them, part branching off to form a loop around the massive grounds while the rest continued on, through the center of it all. Gwen had been attacked, then discovered, on the perimeter loop.

All while Lucas was fast asleep.

Apparently feeling the tension, too, Gwen slipped her hand around his elbow as the fork in the path drew near.

"Look," he said, covering her hand with his. "You used to love this place." He urged her into the grass where a small coffee stand was surrounded by people. A chalkboard listed the daily specials, and garlands of pendants in crimson and gold hung in sweeps from the roof. "You lived on the hot cider and kettle corn for at least half the year," he said, leading her to the back of the line. Their tiny off-campus apartment had smelled of the mouthwatering combination every night when he came home from work. Gwen would be curled on the couch, or face down at her desk, having pressed on in her studies until no amount of sugar and cider could keep her going. Wherever he found her, he'd gather her into his arms, kiss her head and carry her to their bed, eager to slide in beside her.

They shuffled forward with the line, watching each customer walk away with something heavenly scented, a cup, a bag or both. Lucas ordered for them when they reached the counter, sensing Gwen was somewhere else completely. He tucked a tip in the jar, then stepped aside to wait on the drinks. Her gaze was distant and blank. Lost in a memory she likely wouldn't want to share.

"Maybe we can head over to the student center from here," he suggested, pretending not to notice her clear and growing distress. She'd only deny it if he brought it up.

They'd been moving in the direction of her attack site, but they didn't have to go there today, or ever, if she didn't want to. There was plenty of campus left to explore without it, and they had as much time as she needed to do it.

"No," she said softly, turning in his direction. "We should get back on the loop, take it around campus. I want to get that part over with. Then maybe I'll be able to relax, knowing the worst is behind me and I don't have to go back."

"We don't have to go at all," he said. "I have dozens of photos of the area at home. We can go over them together later."

"Photos aren't the same," she said with a sigh. "I can do this. I just have to get past the block in my mind that says it's still dangerous there when I know it's not. The path is safe. The man is dangerous, and he's not here. He's been in my head for years, keeping me from doing things I wanted, but not today. I can take a walk anywhere I want, in broad daylight, with a local lawman, and he can't stop me."

Brave words, he thought, though her expression wasn't selling the sentiment. Any clues that might've been found on the path were long gone, erased by time, weather and foot traffic, but she wanted to face her fears, and he was there to support her.

"You have your gun on you, right?" she asked, a small smile playing on her lips.

Lucas snorted. "Always."

"Good. I'm hoping the walk will trigger a memory we can use to name this guy," she said. "Right now, all I get are flashes of emotion, shocks of fear and single images or phantom pains. Nothing big picture. Nothing substantial." She swallowed hard, then started when the barista called their orders up.

Lucas passed her the cider, and she lifted it to her lips, a small quake in her arms.

Before he could suggest, again, that they go another direction for now, Gwen started down the path. Head high and cider pressed between both palms, she walked on, confident and determined.

He did his best to keep up while also keeping watch. With so many people on campus, it was hard to tell if anyone was looking their way and why. Maybe no one was watching, but he wouldn't be so naive as to assume that ever again.

Gwen's pace slowed as they drew nearer to the site of her attack, and the hairs on the back of Lucas's neck stood at attention. Frantic voices carried around the bend, where a grove of trees met the path and a shallow ravine was lined in river rock.

They both knew the spot too well.

Lucas set a palm against her back, and they hurried to meet the tiny crowd.

Six young faces looked to them as they approached. All women. All early twenties at most, and all with wide eyes and open mouths. When they turned away, their collective gazes fell to the ground before them.

"What's going on?" Lucas asked, stepping ahead and tucking Gwen protectively, instinctively behind him.

"We don't know," a petite brunette said. "It's really creepy. Right? Is it supposed to be a joke? Does it mean something?"

The group loosened their semicircle, revealing the outline of a body painted on the ground. A head drawn over the rocks, arms wide and legs splayed into the grass. A hunting knife stabbed into the heart of the outline pinned a flyer to the ground. The sides flapped, and edges curled in the hearty breeze.

Gwen gasped and stumbled backward. The brunette caught her and the others gathered tightly around, whispering words of comfort and sharing their own fears about what it might mean.

"We called campus security," someone said as Lucas inched over the small incline, snapping on a pair of gloves to avoid contaminating the scene. "SAVE THE DATE" was written across the top of the paper. Bellemont Homecoming across the bottom. Dates were inked in a series of pendants and balloons at the center.

"It doesn't make any sense, right?" a female voice asked from behind him.

"Homecoming is this week," someone else said. "The dates are wrong."

Lucas stretched back onto his feet and flashed his badge to the ladies, while a single tear fell from Gwen's eye. "That was the date of homecoming six years ago. And this is officially a crime scene."

Chapter Thirteen

Gwen perched on the edge of an uncomfortable chair
inside Lucas's office at the West Liberty police station.
It was nearly dinnertime, and she was feeling the weight
of her day in the extreme. She was tired, hungry and
the aspirin she'd taken that morning had long worn off.
Add to that the stress of returning to Bellemont, only to
see a threat had been laid out for her, and she wanted to
scream. Somehow he'd known she would be there. Or
maybe he'd planned for her to be there. After all, his
invitation on her windshield was what had started her
new nightmare. Was it possible the man stalking her
knew her better than she knew herself? Because she'd
only made the decision to go to Bellemont that morning, and it had taken some internal convincing.

Her knees bobbed wildly beneath her as she waited
for Lucas to return once more. He'd been called away
numerous times since their arrival, giving and receiving information on her case. Each consecutive disap-
pearance seemed to wind her nerves more tightly. She
chewed gingerly at the tender skin around her thumbnail, wrangling a mass of ping-ponging thoughts.

She wondered, for example, about the number of strange looks she'd received following Lucas into the station, after a crime scene crew had taken over on campus. The looks might not have been intentional, but there were definitely looks. Curious. Pointed. Looks. Did the lookers know who she was? Had they heard about everything that was going on around her? Or did they assume she was another in Lucas's long line of, allegedly fictional, dates. Not that any of that should matter now.

She freed her tortured thumb and clasped her hands, then released them again in favor of scrubbing her face. She winced when her fingertips hit her goose egg on her forehead. Maybe that was what they'd all been looking at. The entire day had been a train wreck of emotions. The whole week, really. From her suspicions of being followed, to the flyer confirming it, a near abduction, then all this. She leaned forward to wedge her forearms against her bobbing knees and hissed at the burn in her side where stitches closed her recent knife wound.

She closed her eyes and concentrated on her breathing. Deep inhalations. Slow exhalations. And she focused her thoughts on that night, six years ago. If she wanted to help stop her attacker, she needed to remember something useful.

She visualized her closest college friends. Recalled the restaurant where they'd met for dinner and drinks. The squeals and applause when she showed them her engagement ring. She saw the meal. The drinks. And the night's sky as she'd tipped her head back, admiring

FREE BOOKS GIVEAWAY

Complete the survey below and return it today to receive up to 4 FREE BOOKS and FREE GIFTS guaranteed!

FREE BOOKS GIVEAWAY
Reader Survey

1	**2**	**3**
Do you prefer stories with suspenseful storylines?	Do you share your favorite books with friends?	Do you often choose to read instead of watching TV?
◯ YES ◯ NO	◯ YES ◯ NO	◯ YES ◯ NO

YES! Please send me my Free Rewards, consisting of **2 Free Books from each series I select** and **Free Mystery Gifts**. I understand that I am under no obligation to buy anything, as explained on the back of this card.

❏ Harlequin® Romantic Suspense (240/340 HDL GQ3J)
❏ Harlequin Intrigue® Larger-Print (199/399 HDL GQ3J)
❏ Try Both (240/340 & 199/399 HDL GQ3U)

FIRST NAME	LAST NAME

ADDRESS

APT.#	CITY

STATE/PROV.	ZIP/POSTAL CODE

EMAIL ❏ Please check this box if you would like to receive newsletters and promotional emails from Harlequin Enterprises ULC and its affiliates. You can unsubscribe anytime.

the endless stars on her walk home. In those precious moments, everything was right in her world.

Her eyes opened unintentionally, and her thoughts bounced back to the present. The way they always did when she got to this part of the memory.

She dropped her face into waiting palms, pressing her hands hard against closed eyes, and tried again. *Remember*, she ordered herself, falling back to the lost moments.

Her skin went cold, and the flashes began immediately.

Angry eyes. A black balaclava. Pain.

Grass. Trees. Rocks. Blood.

Her eyes opened once more. Protecting herself from what was to come. She struggled to steady her breaths, which were short and ragged. Her body shook with effort, as if remembering was physically exhausting, yet she hadn't managed to do that. Not really.

It had taken her weeks to recall anything at all about that night. She'd successfully, unintentionally, blocked every detail beyond the moment she'd kissed Lucas goodbye. He went to work. She went to meet friends. Her mind had buried everything else in mental concrete, which she'd slowly chipped away at for years. Only recently uncovering a few flashes of images and sounds.

Her therapist had called it progress.

Lucas's voice drew her attention to the door. He cruised inside with drinks. "Sorry that took so long." He set a cup of coffee on his desk, then offered her a bottle of water.

"Thanks."

"But wait," he said, digging into his pocket. "There's more." He produced a two-pack of aspirin and passed them her way.

"Bless." She accepted the offer greedily. "What's going on now?" she asked, popping the pills into her mouth, then washing them down. "You were gone awhile. Did they find something at the scene?" Something that led directly to the man who was ruining her life?

"No." Lucas rested his backside against his desk, stretching long legs between them. "This was something different." He grimaced and shook his head. "I've got a repeat offender I keep arresting, Tommy Black. He likes to get high and assault his girlfriend. I put him in jail again earlier this week, but he made bail. I called to warn his girl, because he sees her as the reason he gets arrested."

Gwen rolled her eyes. "She calls the police, so he says it's her fault?"

"Yep. Well, it's been more than seventy-two hours since he made bail, so I should've expected I'd see him again."

Heat rushed to Gwen's cheeks and her empty stomach heaved. "What does that mean? He hurt her again?"

"Like clockwork," Lucas said. His shoulders were slumped, his expression weary. "I hate this guy, deeply, and there's nothing I can do about him. I make the arrest. He gets off. Wash. Rinse. Repeat. It'd help if the girlfriend would testify against him, but she won't. She calls for help, but that's it. She says it's my job from there, and I just keep failing her."

"She's scared," Gwen said, her throat tightening with the words. "I can't imagine living like that. Face-to-face with a real and present danger every day." The fear of out-of-sight dangers was bad enough. What would it be like to know her monster was coming for her, in the flesh, at every turn? Hurting her again and again.

"Well, it is what it is," Lucas said. "Uniforms picked him up again, and they're hauling him in now. He's extra high, so he's extra obnoxious, aggressive and loud. A real trifecta of fun."

Gwen went back to chewing on her thumbnail. "At least he's been arrested. Is she okay?"

"Hospital." He sighed deeply, then peeled himself away from his desk. "I'm sure she'll be here to plead his case as soon as they release her. I'll have to leave you again for a few minutes when Tommy gets here. They'll rebook him, and I'll get a few minutes for another heart-to-heart. Maybe in his drugged-up state of mind he'll reveal something that leads to an arrest on some other count that won't need the girlfriend's testimony to make stick."

Gwen nodded, feeling the unknown woman's fear and turmoil as if it was her own. "Okay."

A sharp wolf whistle nearly launched her from her chair. The hearty laugh that followed drew a smile over her face.

She angled on her seat to watch the familiar man walk through the door.

Derek Winchester struck a cocky pose before her, all swagger and knockout good looks with a knee-buckling grin. "Well, if it isn't my baby brother's sexy

ex. The fierce and formidable, Gorgeous Gwen Kind."
He winked.

"Knock it off," Lucas complained, motioning his
oldest brother to take a seat.

Derek obliged, lowering his lean body onto the chair
beside hers. He slung a long arm across the back of
her seat.

Her smile grew and her heart danced at the sight of
him. "What are you doing here?" She loved Derek like
a brother. A rebellious, sexy older brother. One who'd
always taken her side when she and Lucas debated anything. Whatever Derek could do to ruffle his family's
feathers, he was on it. Like becoming a private detective
instead of just joining the force like his dad, granddad
and great-granddad before him.

In hindsight, maybe it wasn't such a leap for Lucas
to have traded architecture for law enforcement. Some
might argue it was in his blood. Though, she'd never
gotten the idea anyone expected him to do anything in
life other than what he wanted. And Lucas had never
said anything to make her think he was interested in
carrying a badge.

Derek looked her over, long and slow. "I heard you
were here, and I had to come and see for myself." His
gaze lingered at the ugly purple-and-black knot on her
head. "I heard you've had a rough couple of days." He
cast a look in Lucas's direction.

"Who told?" she asked.

"Blaze."

"Ah," she said. That made perfect sense. Blaze was
their middle brother, a homicide detective at the pre-

cinct. One she hoped she'd see again soon. The circumstances were awful, but being there with Lucas and Derek felt a bit like an odd family reunion, and she liked it.

Lucas pulled his phone into view and bobbed his head as he read the screen. "The guys are here with Tommy Black. I need to take care of that. You good?" he asked, flicking his gaze from Gwen to Derek, then back.

She nodded and smiled.

Lucas walked away slowly. "Don't listen to anything Derek says," he instructed.

And Derek's smile widened. "How are you holding up?" he asked, once Lucas had vanished.

"I'm getting through it," she said.

"You always do." He cocked his head and stretched back on his seat. "I wish I could say I'm sorry all this is happening."

"You're not?" she asked, frowning despite herself.

"Nah. If this guy wasn't at it again, and coming about things the way he is, he might never be arrested for what he did to you. Now, it's only a matter of time. Heck, Lucas might even let me help him now. Being a PI has its privileges you know. I don't have to abide by all the same rules and regulations my brothers do. I can go a little rogue, as needed. It's a perk of the trade."

"Uh-huh." Gwen's smile returned as she ran over his words with hope. "You really think he'll be caught this time?"

"I'm sure of it. He messed up when he made himself known. Whatever drove him to it is the same thing that's going to be his downfall." Derek's phone buzzed inside his pocket, and he took it out for a look at the screen. "Duty calls," he said. "I'm on the job, but I had to stop and say welcome back. You're in good hands with Lucas. No one loves you like my brother."

She stood to see Derek to the door, then fell easily into his embrace when he offered one. The second hug, from a man, in less than twenty-four hours, and once again she was surprised by how easy and natural it felt. Though, Derek was much more than some man. He'd nearly been her brother-in-law, and he'd always been her champion. "See you," she said, as he winked his goodbye.

She leaned against the doorjamb, watching him leave and wondering if it could really be so simple to fall back into her previous life. Would everyone be as accepting as Lucas, Isaac and Derek? Surely not, but wouldn't it be worth the meddlesome individuals who weren't if it meant she could be back here again…permanently?

Her ears perked at the sounds of distant shouts and commotion. Derek broke into a jog at the end of the hall, heading through the lobby door, toward whatever was happening.

Thumps, crashes and curses grew louder by the second, and Gwen leaned forward, senses on high alert and ready to run. She wasn't sure where she'd run, but the adrenaline was already building.

"Tommy Black!" Lucas's voice rose above the others, cut short as the door closed behind Derek.

Gwen stepped into the hall, a small measure of relief soothing the growing panic. The source of the problem was a conflict between Lucas and his criminal nemesis. Not her personal monster come to make good on his threat drawn in the campus grass.

A few steps from the door separating offices and interrogation rooms from the lobby, a thunderous boom erupted, and her muscles locked down.

Derek's face appeared outside the rectangular window in the door, eyes wide and expression hard. "Lucas!"

Gwen's world tilted. Her frozen muscles released, and she ran. Not away from the danger, but to it. The booming sound echoed in her heart and head. A gunshot? *No. Not that*, she thought. *Please, not that*. She couldn't lose Lucas again. Not now.

She burst into the lobby where a pack of officers had circled up, staring at the floor while a man in cuffs thrashed and kicked against his detaining officer. The thug landed a few kicks as others in uniform tried to still him. The mob shifted, and a large metal cabinet came into view, toppled onto the tile floor beside Lucas, glaring at the man in cuffs as blood rushed from his nose and lip.

Gwen nearly laughed in relief. Lucas was fine. He'd possibly been the recipient of one of Tommy Black's wild kicks, but he wasn't shot, and he would heal. She tugged on the door she'd exited, only to find it locked, of course. She'd have to wait until an officer headed back inside. So, she sidestepped a clutch of lawmen, attempting to stay out of everyone's way, and thankful the mess before her was something the police could handle.

"Tommy!" A woman wailed, pulling Gwen's attention toward the ladies' room door. The woman raced

forward, into the mix of flailing feet and shouting officers. Tears streamed over bruised cheeks, falling from
two black eyes. "Baby! I'm sorry," she cried, colliding
with the man directly at Tommy's back and attempting
to pry his arms off her man.

Tommy seemed to recognize her voice amid the
chaos, and he jerked toward it, nearly tossing her and
the man behind him off their feet.

She pleaded for Tommy's forgiveness as Derek
caught her by the arms and pulled her back.

Tommy screamed every awful thing Gwen had ever
heard at the woman, and then some more.

All the while, the station's front doors opened and
closed with the arrival and departure of visitors and officers. Some in suits. Some in uniforms.

Gwen pressed herself to the wall, waiting for it all
to end.

When another criminal was hauled in wearing cuffs,
Tommy seemed to double down on his efforts for free-
dom, and gooseflesh rose over Gwen's arms.

The incoming criminal took Tommy's lead and
began to buck and fight. His elbow landed in the doughy
gut of his detaining officer, and the older man jack-
knifed forward, releasing his hold. The female officer
manning the desk leaped into action, chasing the run-
away man in cuffs, and the chaos doubled.

A scalding wet collision stole Gwen's breath, and for
a moment, she thought she'd been attacked. A middle-
aged man in a suit stared wide-eyed. His coffee cup now
empty. Its contents thrown over Gwen's chest and face.

"I am so sorry," he said, genuinely horrified. "I was

shoved." He looked behind him, but no one was there. "I'm sorry," he repeated, pulling a white linen handkerchief from his pocket.

"I'm okay," she said, plucking the material of her turtleneck away from her chest and waving off the handkerchief. For the first time in hours, she really was okay. "Excuse me." She ducked into the restroom Tommy's girlfriend had exited, then checked under every stall for good measure.

A smile bloomed over her face in another rush of relief. Lucas was fine. She was fine. And everything else would be fine very soon. Derek believed that, and she would believe him, too.

She tore a handful of paper towels from the dispenser then thrust them under cold water, prepared to do what she could for her cream turtleneck and jean jacket. And planning to take her time until the lobby quieted, and she could ask to be let back inside the main building.

She lifted her gaze to the mirror, wet towels pressed to her chest.

And saw the masked man's reflection in the mirror only a moment before his hands curved around her neck from behind, and he began to squeeze.

Chapter Fourteen

Lucas ambled back down the hall to his office. His nose throbbed, and if it wasn't broken, it'd be a miracle. A slow smile spread over his face at the thought. That would make two miracles, because his first was that Tommy Black officially assaulted an officer. Six officers, actually, while high, angry and extremely disorderly. He'd threatened to kill all the injured cops, blow up the station, murder his girlfriend and a slew of other vicious things while on camera. So, Anise would finally be safe, at least for a little while, because Tommy would definitely get some real jail time now. With or without her testimony.

He swung into his office with an apologetic grin. "Sorry that took so long."

The rest of the words stalled on his tongue. His office was empty.

He went back into the hall. "Gwen?" he called, looking in both directions before heading toward the officers' restrooms and vestibule with vending machines. He knocked on the bathroom door, then pressed it open an inch. "Gwen?"

"What are you doing?" Derek asked, dropping change into the vending machine.

"Looking for Gwen." He fought against a swell of panic, urging himself to be sensible. She hadn't been abducted inside a police station. "I thought you had work to do."

"I do, and what do you mean, looking for Gwen?" Derek asked, retrieving an ice-cold soda and handing it to his brother. "For your face."

Lucas held the can to his swollen nose. "She's not in my office or the ladies' room. Where was she when you left her?"

"In your office," Derek said, concern changing his usually smug expression.

"Check around back. Find someone who saw her leave my office. I'm heading to the lobby. If there's any chance she was taken outside during all that racket, it'll be caught on camera."

Derek broke left, heading toward the nearby desks and offices.

Lucas made a run for the lobby. He pushed through the automatically locking security door, then cut past the handful of people waiting to sign in. "Hey," he called, sliding in beside the next guest and drawing the young female officer's attention. "The woman I had in my office, Gwen Kind, have you seen her?"

Lanie frowned. She had an ice pack against her swollen cheek and a scowl on her face. "Your guy Black sure caused a hell of a lot of trouble out here. He kicked me in the face when I tried to keep Banister's guy from running out the front door."

Lucas straightened, raking frustrated hands through his hair. "Gwen's missing, and she's in danger," he said. "I need to know she wasn't taken during the chaos. Buzz me in to look at the security feed."

Lanie buzzed him through the door separating her from the lobby. Her scowl melted into something more like shock. "The redhead? You think that's possible?"

He froze, snapping his attention to her. "Why? Did you see her?" Heat crawled up his neck and over his face. If Lanie had seen Gwen in the lobby, she'd been only a few yards from the front door.

"I think so. She was out here when I went to assist Banister."

"Then what?" he asked.

"I don't know. I subdued the guy, got kicked in the face on my way back. I didn't see much other than spots after that."

Lucas cursed. He turned in a small circle, then hunched over her desk, accessing the surveillance feed and rewinding by several minutes, to the start of the brawl.

"You think she's gone-gone?" she asked. "Taken during all the commotion?"

His chest constricted with rage and fear at the possibility. "Maybe."

"Pardon me." A shadow fell over the counter between them, and a middle-aged man in a suit smiled apologetically. "I'm sorry to bother you," he said. "I'm attorney David Neils, and I wonder if you're talking about the same redheaded woman I ran into? Midtwenties? Curly hair?"

"You saw her?" Lucas asked, fumbling for his phone. He accessed a photo he'd taken that morning and thrust the device in Neils's direction. Her red hair looked like fire, lifting and blowing alongside the colorful campus leaves.

"Yes. That's her." He looked sheepish again. "I spilled my coffee on her when someone shoved me during the brouhaha," he said. "She went into the restroom."

"Alone?" Lucas demanded, heading back through the security door to the lobby.

"Yes. I think so."

"Did you see her come out?" he asked, around the corner and darting for the public ladies' room. He swung the door wide without waiting for an answer. Intuition spiked in his chest, and he knew.

He'd failed her again.

AIR RUSHED INTO Gwen's lungs with a whoosh and a burn. Her body jolted upright on the cold floor, and tears flowed immediately from her eyes. Her heart raced with the knowledge something awful had happened, but it was several moments before the actual memories returned.

"Gwen?" The bathroom door swung open, banging against the wall and ricocheting off.

She started at the sound, but couldn't speak, still trapped in the horrific and detailed memory of her stalker's hands around her throat. His crazed eyes in the mirror's reflection. His breath in her hair.

He'd gotten to her in the police station bathroom with a half-dozen officers just outside the door.

Self-pity climbed to the forefront of emotions in her heart and took roost. The awful why-is-this-happening-to-me soundtrack began to play, and she let go as the desperation she'd barely kept under control all day broke free. She needed to get help. Needed to get up, but her body shook and her legs were weak and useless, as she tugged them tightly to her chest.

"Gwen?" Lucas fell to his knees before her, hands hovering, wanting to touch, but not daring. Extra careful because he saw through her pretenses and facades. Lucas saw what she worked so hard to hide from everyone else. He saw all her broken pieces.

She gasped, having forgotten to breathe, and her throat burned anew.

Derek appeared, barely a heartbeat behind Lucas, kicking open stalls and rising on tiptoes to peer through the undamaged glass block window high on the wall. "What happened?"

Her stalker had choked her. He'd watched her struggle in the mirror until spots had danced in her vision, and her frantic hands had fallen away from his arms. Then he'd changed his hold, offering her air while she was too fatigued and dizzy to fight. And as she'd gulped for breath, he'd applied pressure to her neck in a new way, winding an arm under her chin in a choke hold. He'd pressed the veins that carried blood away from her brain until her world had gone black. And she'd thought for sure he'd finally done it. After all she'd done to survive, he'd finally finished what he started and killed her.

Lucas leaned closer, palms up and expression flat. "Hey," he urged, fighting her thoughts back to the moment. "Can you hear me?"

She nodded, wiping hot tears from her cheeks. Tears would do no good now.

"Can I help you up? Are you able to stand?" he asked, keen eyes evaluating.

She wasn't sure, but she loosened her grip on her knees, willing to try. Anything to get out of that bathroom.

"Did you get a look at this guy?" Derek asked. "Did he say anything?"

Gwen clutched on to Lucas, forcing her trembling body to cooperate. A sob tore from her chest at the memory, ripping up her aching throat. "He said, go home. Go. Home. Go. Home," she whispered just as her attacker had while she'd slowly lost consciousness.

Lucas wrapped an arm around her back and held her tight as she worked to get her feet under her. "I'm so sorry," he whispered back.

Derek held the door for them as they shuffled away from the restroom.

Several sets of curious eyes watched as they emerged. She could only imagine what she looked like, and she didn't want to know. Blaze Winchester's narrow-eyed stare was among the onlookers. "Gwen?"

The three brothers exchanged a look, trading silent information in the curious way they always had, then they parted ways. Lucas hauled Gwen slowly toward the parking lot. Derek stayed behind, explaining the situation to Blaze.

The air was brisk outside, and she shivered in response. The sun had set on another awful day, spreading shades of twilight across the land. "Where are we going?" she asked. Her addled mind worked to make sense of leaving the station. "I need to make a report."

"You need medical attention." Lucas guided her to his truck, then helped her inside. "You can make a statement when we know you're okay," he said, eyes compassionate and jaw locked. "We're going to the hospital to get you checked out. Blaze will take over inside. He'll get the team to comb the ladies' room for anything left behind we can use to identify who did this to you. Lanie is probably already reviewing the video feeds. They've got that, and I've got you."

Lucas closed her door and rounded the hood to the driver's side. He started the engine and waited while she buckled up.

Every movement felt slow and complicated, like moving through molasses. Almost surreal. She blinked wet eyes as she trailed her fingertips along the tender skin of her neck. "He could have killed me," she whispered. "I thought he did. Why didn't he?"

Lucas shifted the truck into gear and motored away from the station. He stole a glance at her before pulling onto the road. "Have you ever seen a cat with a mouse? Everything they put them through? They lose interest once the mouse stops running."

Her throat tightened, and another tear fell unbidden as she heard her attacker's voice in her ear. *Go. Home. Go. Home.* He couldn't take her away, through a lobby filled with officers, and he couldn't stalk her properly with Lucas always at her side. So, he'd wanted her to go home.

She wouldn't be any fun to him if she was dead.

GWEN WOKE AGAIN late that night. With the hospital behind her once more, she'd fallen fast asleep in Lucas's bed. Fatigue had dragged her quickly under, and she'd slept soundly until the clattering of cups and plates had nudged her awake. A round of low voices rose through the old cavernous home. Four voices. And she recognized them all. Lucas. Derek. Blaze and Isaac Winchester.

She climbed out of bed and tugged a hooded sweatshirt over the T-shirt and yoga pants she'd chosen for pajamas, then headed downstairs.

The tangy scent of pizza sauce mixed with salty aromas of pepperoni and cheese in the air. Black coffee underscored it all.

The voices quieted as she padded across the foyer in socked feet, down the hall to the kitchen. The men turned her way as she took the final step into view.

Lucas was out of his chair in the next breath, meeting her where she was and ushering her to his empty seat at the table. "Here." He offered her a bottle of water from the collection of food and drinks on the table. Soda bottles, paper plates and napkins sat with pizza boxes and chips. "Coffee's on if you'd rather have that. Are you hungry?"

"Water's fine." She gave the food before her a regretful look, then frowned. She was hungry, but couldn't imagine attempting to swallow anything from the selection on the table. Not with her throat as badgered as it had been.

"I made soup," he said. "It's in the fridge. I can heat it when you're ready."

"Okay," she said. "Thank you." Her stomach gurgled at the promise of sustenance, and Lucas smiled.

"Give me two minutes."

The remaining Winchesters stared at her from their places around the table. Isaac with his evaluating eyes. Derek with his clenched fists. And Blaze with curiosity and regret, likely calculating how this had happened and what the next step would be.

She lifted a palm to them in a half-hearted wave.

"Hey," they mumbled back, each sounding a little guilty for something that was nowhere near their fault.

"Welcome back," Blaze said wryly. "Wondering why you ever left?"

Her lips tugged into a tiny smile. "Every minute. So, what were you all talking about before I interrupted?"

"You," he answered softly, honestly.

She'd expected as much. "Did the crime scene team find anything useful at the scene on campus or in the bathroom at the police station?" she asked. "Did you get him on camera entering or leaving the building?"

"Nothing from campus," Blaze said. "There are just too many people over there to isolate tracks or trace evidence for one individual. Bathroom was clean, too. Surveillance cameras cover all entrances and exits at the station, so we definitely got him. Problem is we don't know who we're looking for, and there were a lot of people coming and going while Tommy Black was causing trouble."

"No one noticed a man coming out of the ladies room?" she asked, heart falling with the question. Obviously not, or they would have told her already. "So, he got away again."

Derek drummed his thumbs along the table's edge. "Not completely and not forever. We have signatures from every visitor who signed in and out today. Once we compare the names to the faces caught on film, we can pare them down. Of those, one is likely linked to your past somehow."

"Okay," she said, breaking the word into halves. "So, he's definitely on video, but unlikely to have signed in. Maybe I can check the videos for familiar faces. Odds are I know him, right? We probably met before he started to follow me?"

Blaze and Derek exchanged a look.

"What?" Gwen pressed. "Tell me."

Blaze shifted, pulling her attention from Derek. "One of the officers wrestling with Tommy Black blocked the lobby camera that has a view of the restrooms in its scope. We can see someone leave, but can't see his face. We can guess his height, but little else. He seemed to be wearing a black coat, but nothing that stood out. Then, the crowd shifts and he goes out of frame. He becomes visible again outside, but he leaves with a group being asked to wait there while officers move Tommy Black and Banister's guy out of the lobby and over to processing. Our guy doesn't wait with the rest. He keeps walking until he's out of view again."

"So, he's familiar with your setup?" she guessed. An icy chill rolled through her core. "A cop?"

"No," Blaze and Derek answered together.

Isaac's kind eyes crinkled at the corners, clearly amused. "Lots of people visit the station. Cleaning crews, delivery people, maintenance, lawyers, visitors of detainees, criminals." He let the last word stick.

"Of course," she agreed sheepishly.

Lucas returned to her with a steaming bowl and settled it before her on the table. A spoon and napkin at its side.

The warm, buttery scents excited her stomach, which she realized had been empty for hours. "Thank you."

He dragged a stool into the space beside her and sat, watching as she managed the first hot spoonful. "We've been working with our profilers on this guy," he said. "Don't give up hope just yet. Even if we can't get a look at his face, we can generate a mold based on his behaviors this week that will help narrow the suspect pool."

Gwen had given her statement at the hospital, but it hadn't been much. Her attacker was tall. Same black balaclava as always. Same angry eyes and violent hands.

"We assume he's an outdoorsman," Lucas began. "He was comfortable spending hours on the ground among the trees at the hike-and-bike trail, watching for you. He owns a high-caliber ghillie suit and knew how to use it to his full advantage in the woods. Your original attack was outdoors, also. Some criminals would have followed you home that night, where there were walls to shield sound and view. He didn't do that. Maybe because he knew you spent most nights with me. Maybe because he prefers to be outside."

Blaze pointed to Lucas in agreement, but clearly with something to add. "This guy was patient in his stalking. Painfully so. Unrushed for at least two years before the first attack. And we know he kept watch for six years afterward. He has a job with a flexible schedule, and given the number of photos taken in public spaces, he moves through society unnoticed."

Gwen struggled to keep up, but her mind had hooked on the word *outdoorsman*. It was a polite way to summarize him, but her stalker was much more than that. Lucas just hadn't wanted to say the more accurate and on-the-nose word in his mind.

Hunter.

She thought back to the analogy he'd made in the truck about the cat and its mouse. Her stalker was a hunter, and she was being hunted.

Lucas looked pained as he watched her processing the profile. "We think his patience only lasts as long as he feels in control. You never knew he was there until he wanted you to know. So, we can assume something changed to make him want to scare you this time. Something made him feel as if he was losing control of his fantasy. Based on timing, we can guess that our engagement was the catalyst before."

Gwen considered the notion of letting the punishment fit the crime. "You think his reaction was extreme because marrying you would have been permanent."

"Possibly," Lucas said. "He was younger. Newer at this. Age and maturity could have been a factor in him losing control, or there could have been another factor in his life that had him already on the edge."

His brothers grunted their agreement.

"Unfortunately, there's no real profile for rapists," Lucas went on, speaking gently, but factually. "These are all just guesses, but it would explain the extreme violence and timing of the first attack. Presumably his attempt to assert control and ownership over the object of his obsession. You."

Gwen abandoned the spoon in her soup. Her arms wound protectively around her center. "Ownership?"

Lucas nodded, emotion thick in his cool blue eyes. "The profilers at the precinct will have a more complete profile soon, but they say someone who's devoted so many years of his life to watching you probably believes he's part of yours. He's invested."

"He thinks he's part of my life," she echoed. "He's what? Delusional? Had a psychotic break?"

Lucas offered the saddest of smiles. "Extreme stalkers are often delusional in that regard. He probably imagines himself at the restaurant tables with you and your friends. Jogging beside you in the mornings. Curled on the couch with you at night. And in those moments, he's happy. And so are you. Together."

She pressed her lips tight, unable to stop the shudder rocking through her. "And when I accepted your proposal, I rejected him. A husband would have ruined his fantasy."

Blaze dipped his chin. "That's the working theory."

"Okay." She took a breath to center herself. "So, what upset him this time?"

"You tell us," Blaze said. "The infringements started small and in your town. Small punishments for a small infraction, likely. You came back to West Liberty, and the behaviors escalated."

Gwen's eyes fell slowly shut. "I came back to Lucas. The man I'd planned to marry." She peeled her eyes open with a groan. "But what did I do to deserve the small punishments back home? I haven't done anything unusual. I jog. Go to work. Go home. Same old. Everyday. Sometimes I get drinks or dinner with the ladies from the office, but not often, and I've been doing that for years."

The men didn't look convinced.

Derek kicked back in his chair. "Something changed."

"If not with you, then with him," Blaze agreed.

Gwen looked to Lucas. "Nothing. I swear."

Lucas heaved a sigh and raked his fingers through his hair. "We'll figure it out."

Gwen returned to her soup, running mentally over the past few weeks. Reviewing the days before the flyer arrived on her windshield. Had something changed?

She set the spoon down again. "Collin."

Lucas tensed beside her. Whatever he'd been saying to his brother was cut off at the sound of her voice. "Who?"

She covered her mouth, unsure how she hadn't thought of him before, while wondering if she was completely off base. "There's a man at work," she began. "He's an architect at the firm. He walks me to my car at night." She grimaced, recalling the big deal her co-workers made of it. "He's asked me out a couple of times, as friends. For a drink or dinner after work, but I don't go," she assured him. She'd considered accepting his offer more than once, but she couldn't. Collin was a good guy, and he deserved a normal, uncomplicated person in his life. Gwen had stopped being normal the moment a psychopath had decided to hunt her.

Did her stalker know Collin? How else could he know about the flirting and invitations?

And then she remembered.

"I had dinner with him." Her eyes widened at the recollection. "We went for drinks as a group, but everyone else left before ordering any food. He and I had nowhere to be and were talking about ideas for a new client, so we stayed."

"How long ago was that?" Lucas asked.

"A few weeks." Right before she'd started feeling watched.

That accidental dinner had set her nightmare back in motion.

Chapter Fifteen

Lucas cleared the breakfast dishes, tired from a long night of rehashing ugly details with Gwen and his brothers. He'd barely slept afterward, and when he had, he'd woken to images of Gwen being choked out. In his dreams, she didn't wake up. And every time, he'd found his way to her bedroom to be sure she was still okay. He'd made the trip so many times before dawn, he'd considered sleeping in the hallway outside her door. Ultimately, he'd stuck it out in the guest room across the hall, door open and hypertuned to her every deep breath and rustle of blankets.

Now, on his fourth cup of coffee and her second mug of tea, they'd passed the morning in companionable silence, more lost in thoughts than conversation.

"Any luck?" he asked, moving to sit with her on his couch in the study. He should've known he'd find her curled up among the books. It was his favorite room in the house. He'd practically lived out of it while he'd renovated the rest of the home, undoing all the awful and occasionally unsound updates that had been made over the years. Thankfully no one had dared touch the study. It was architectural perfection without need of anything more. Grand built-in bookcases soared floor-to-ceiling on his left and right, flanking an expansive set of windows in the exterior wall. It was impossible not to marvel at the extensive detail and craftsmanship of everything in sight. He'd even salvaged the historic stained glass pendant chandelier hanging high above.

She shifted when she saw him, tucking her slender legs beneath her and setting her phone aside. "Not yet." Her bruised head was losing its knot, but the sickly shades of green and yellow made the healing mark look even worse. The dark marks on her neck were another story. "Collin hasn't responded to my texts from last night, and he didn't answer when I tried him again a few minutes ago. I'm starting to worry." She lifted the teapot from a tray on the coffee table before her and refilled her cup. "What if something's happened to him because of me?"

"Let's not worry until there's a reason to worry," Lucas said. "Remember. We're running on theories. Trying to troubleshoot and get ahead of this mess somehow." Not an easy task when they didn't know anything about the stalker's life or personality beyond his obsession with Gwen. Lucas took a long swig of coffee, then set the mug aside. "I have an idea." He turned his phone over and brought up the number to the design firm where Gwen and Collin worked, then dialed. "Maybe I can catch him at the office."

Gwen frowned. "I hate to bother him at work. Especially if we're wrong." She sighed, raising her teacup higher and inhaling deeply. "Honestly, I hate to tell him anything about this at all." She tucked wild red curls behind her ear a moment before they sprang free. She repeated the effort immediately, earning the same result. "He'll likely freak out and ask my coworkers if they know anything about my past or my absence beyond what you told my boss after the copier incident. No one knows anything, so they'll all go to the internet, if they haven't already, and just like that." She paused to snap her fingers. "All my carefully laid plans to keep the past and present from mixing are ruined."

Lucas shook his head. "I hate to break it to you, but your past and present have been mixing for years. You just didn't know it until recently. You haven't done anything wrong, so whoever finds out about what you've been through will just have to deal with it and get over it. However complicated that might feel to them, it doesn't hold a candle to what you've been through. What you're going through," he corrected.

The call finally connected, and a woman answered.

"This is Detective Winchester, West Liberty PD," he explained. "I'd like to speak with Collin…" He looked to Gwen, realizing too late that he didn't know her friend's last name.

"Weinstein," she said, filling in the missing name.

"Collin Weinstein," Lucas repeated.

The receptionist put him on hold, and he smiled at Gwen. "She's putting me through."

Ten minutes later, Lucas hung up, having provided Collin with an incredibly loose rundown on the situation. He'd left out the details of what happened to Gwen six years ago, because she was right, that was personal and irrelevant to Collin or anyone else. Instead, Lucas had concentrated on the possibility Collin's dinner with Gwen had provoked her stalker and launched him into action. Gwen had been targeted repeatedly this week, and Collin could possibly be next.

Gwen breathed easier when Lucas disconnected the call. "What did he say?" she asked, having hung visibly on every word from Lucas's mouth. "He's okay? Not hurt or abducted. So, why didn't he answer my calls?"

Lucas fought the pinch of rejection and jealousy her concern for Collin created. Gwen had only returned to Lucas's life out of necessity, he reminded himself. They weren't in love anymore, and it would do him good to remember that. "He said it was late when you messaged him last night, and he's been busy at work this morning, but he planned to return your call during his lunch break." Lucas traded his phone for the cooling coffee and sipped to hide a frown. "He also said he dropped by your house to check on you after word got out about the copier incident. You weren't home. Does he stop by your place often?" Lucas asked, hoping she couldn't hear the intense curiosity in his words.

"No. Never. I didn't even know he knew where I lived," she said. "I guess he asked Marina." She touched a fingertip to her bruised forehead and frowned. "I hate being seen as a victim." Her wide brown eyes narrowed. "I know that's silly and petty in the face of everything else, but I really hate it." She sighed. "I'm trying to remind myself that everything is a matter of perspective. I'm still alive. That's good. And my attacker has gone from bold to flat-out reckless, which is strangely good, as well. He'll be caught for sure if he keeps that up. Right?"

The hope in her eyes nearly stole his breath. He couldn't keep letting her down. "Yes. And you did the right thing by making sure Collin had the facts he needed to stay safe. Even if nothing comes of it, it was good to let him know there was a possibility of danger out there. Now he can be more vigilant and let us know if anything strikes him as odd." Better to tell him the truth and nothing happen, than to tell him nothing and he's ambushed. "You'd never forgive yourself if he was hurt and you hadn't told him to be careful. You've got a big heart. This is just one more way it shows."

She sat straighter at the compliment, and an odd expression washed over her face. "I helped on a school hotline freshman year," she said. "I completely forgot. It didn't last, so it wasn't part of a lasting routine or anything, but for a few weeks, I tried helping strangers that way." Her gaze went distant with the memory. "The callers struggled with loneliness, homesickness and feelings of isolation. I thought I could help because I was going through something similar, so I signed up."

"Did any of the male callers you spoke with seem attached? Did you have repeat callers? Anyone who asked for you by name, perhaps?" Lucas asked, inspecting her beautiful face as it crumpled in thought.

"I don't think so, and we didn't exchange names. That was against the rules." She marveled a moment, lost in thought. "It feels like a lifetime ago. So much has happened since."

"I don't even remember a hotline," Lucas said. "Was it advertised campus-wide?"

"No. It wasn't a Bellemont-sponsored project, but there were flyers on the community boards in the student center, library and common areas."

"Did you take the calls at the counseling center?"

"No, in the psychology department. The hotline was a short-lived research project for a grad student's thesis on loneliness in highly populated spaces and small communities like college campuses. The lines were set up for temporary research, though some of the volunteers thought the school might implement the number permanently if there was a large enough response. There wasn't. The whole thing was done and over before the semester's end." She finished her tea, then set the cup aside once more. "I suppose it's possible that someone I helped on a call became attached. Being lonely is rough. It can play with your self-esteem, your emotions and your mind. Even one friendly person can make all the difference."

Lucas rubbed eager hands against the denim on his thighs. There was something to this worth looking into, but they needed a string to pull. "Was there a staff member overseeing the project?" The grad student was likely long gone by now, but maybe the teacher assigned to the project was still around. "If we're lucky the teacher might remember something worth knowing."

"I loved the teacher. She taught social psychology, I think. She was the nicest woman. She might've even been head of the department at the time," Gwen said.

Lucas brought up a search engine on his cell phone

and found the Bellemont staff directory. He scrolled to the list of names in the psychology department, then handed the phone to Gwen. "Any of those look familiar?"

"Bloomsbury," Gwen said, tapping the screen with her fingertip. An image of an older woman in a black suit jacket and white blouse smiled back. "That's her. She had longer hair then, and it was darker, but that's her."

Lucas took the phone with a grin. "I'll give her a call."

He dialed, waited, then left a voice mail. "I'll follow up with an email," he said, thinking out loud as he went. "And I'll let her know we're coming in to see her during her office hours." He dared a look in Gwen's direction when he finished. He probably should've asked her if she felt up to another trip to the college before volunteering her appearance, but she always had the option of saying no. Or changing her mind at any time. "Feel up to another trip to Bellemont?" he asked, hoping she would agree.

Gwen had the relationship with this professor, not him, and being back in the building might help Gwen recall more details about her time on the hotline and the people she spoke with while she was there. Not to mention the fact that he refused to leave her alone anywhere again. So, if he was going, she was going, and there wasn't a better team for the job.

"Absolutely," she said. "I wouldn't miss it." She pushed slowly to her feet, a small grimace tugging her lips. "I'm going to get showered and dressed. I'll reheat the kettle for tea when I get back and maybe take a couple more aspirins."

"How about you just take your time and enjoy your shower," Lucas suggested. "The tea will be ready when you are."

Gwen smiled. "Thank you." She tipped carefully at the hips and pressed a light kiss to his head, then she was gone.

Lucas moved to the doorway, longing to call to her. To ask her what the kiss was for, and if she'd like to do it again. But he knew the kiss had cost her. After what she'd been through, every physical touch had a price. Lucas worked with rape survivors every day, and he knew how hard the simple gesture had been. He also knew it had taken serious thought and much motivation for her to do it.

He smiled as he crossed the room to his desk and powered up his laptop. He searched for information on the hotline project, hoping the grad student had published a paper on the topic. If he or she had, it wasn't available online. Lucas was sure, however, that if the published paper existed, it would be available in the Bellemont library. A special second-floor section of the library was dedicated to papers, studies and books published by faculty, alumni and staff. Until then, he'd have to wait and wonder.

He scrubbed a palm against his stubble-covered cheeks. He needed a list of people who'd used the hotline number while Gwen had been working there. A line like this would likely have been confidential, but it was also a research project, so there was a chance that some amount of information had been collected for the purpose of documentation. It'd take a warrant to get the details legally, if the teacher wasn't sharing, but that wouldn't be a problem. Finding information on a defunct temporary research project from six years ago was the problem.

Lucas pushed back in his chair, frustration growing. When he thought of all that this lunatic had taken away from Gwen. From him. From the future they'd been planning. Every bit of rage he'd experienced over the years pressed hard against his nerves, willing him to act. He'd love nothing more than to lash out at Gwen's attacker, to let him feel what it was like to be over-powered and afraid, beaten unconscious by a practical stranger. Unfortunately for Lucas's rage and fortunately for her attacker, Lucas wasn't that guy.

He dropped the darker thoughts he'd entertained many times before, and pushed onto his feet instead. He was a good cop, a tenacious detective and an honorable man. Integrity was important to him, and it was what separated Lucas from the men he handcuffed. Gwen deserved more than another angry man in her life. She needed a protector, a partner and a friend.

Lucas was exactly that guy.

Chapter Sixteen

Gwen climbed down from the cab of Lucas's pickup, back on campus and determined to follow this new potential lead as far as possible. She'd do whatever it took to find the man who'd watched her gasp for air while he choked her. His eyes had been more cold than angry this time. His movements more intentional and calculated. Had he made her believe he'd kill her for the sick thrill of it? Had he enjoyed watching her fight frantically, helplessly, then lose, falling limp in his arms, defeated? Or maybe it was all just to prove a point. He was great and mighty and worthy of being feared. While she was a lamb waiting for slaughter. Whatever his motivation and ultimate goal had been, she was willing to bet he hadn't accounted for something else.

Like the fact that she'd reached her tipping point.

He'd taken his attempts to keep her afraid too far. He'd made her believe he'd killed her. And really, what was left to fear beyond death? That he'd really kill her next time? Well, it had felt pretty real this time. She'd already been through the scariest parts, and she was done being afraid of him.

Somewhere between the police station bathroom and Lucas's house, she'd become unnaturally numb. And it had started to seem as if the things happening around her weren't actually happening to her. A protective response from her psyche, no doubt, to keep her from losing her mind, but that was fine by her. The change made her feel brave again.

"You sure you're up to this?" Lucas asked, closing the passenger door for her and pressing the button on his key to lock up. "If you change your mind, we can leave anytime you want."

"I'm okay," she said, smiling for good measure. *Okay* wasn't exactly the right word, but she was ready.

Lucas moved in close, looking pained and unsure. His intensity had reached an all-time high, and it was fighting against her newfound calm.

The muscles in his jaw ticked, and lines raced across his handsome brow as he stared into her eyes. Debating. Scrutinizing. "I have a request," he said finally. "I'm not sure you're going to like it, but I want you to consider. If you say no, I won't ask again," he added.

Her core tensed and her fingers curled into fists inside her warm coat pockets.

Something had Lucas on edge, and he was rarely anything except calm.

She shifted from foot to foot as she waited for him to ask his question. Whatever he wanted, she could handle it. She was strong. And she trusted Lucas. So, how bad could the request be? Did he want to use her as stalker bait? To lure the lunatic out? Would Lucas suggest she let her attacker get his hands on her again so the police could make their arrest? Her stomach lurched at the thought of his touch. "Go on," she said finally, urging Lucas to spit it out.

A gust of sudden wind whipped past, spinning throngs of fallen leaves into a series of little tornadoes along the sidewalk. Lucas's overgrown hair lashed across his forehead, making him look wild and surprisingly youthful. "I think we should hold hands," he said. "As often as possible, while we're on campus or anywhere outside my truck or home."

Gwen barked a laugh, overcome with relief. "You want to hold hands?"

"Yeah," he nodded, looking baffled by her response. "I know it might be uncomfortable for you, but it will help me keep you within reach."

"It'll make you feel better?" she asked, her smile growing. "You've been trying to ask me if you can hold my hand?"

He shrugged, finally joining her in the smile.

Gwen pulled her hands from her pockets and offered them both to him. She'd lost her gloves since her last trip to campus, and was glad on a number of levels for the warmth of his touch.

"I only need one," he said, deliberating before making a choice. "Okay. This one." He made a show of interlocking their fingers before moving forward.

Gwen bit into her lower lip as the familiar jolt of electricity coursed through her at his touch. Then she kept pace thinking of nothing else.

They moved swiftly to the Garber building where the bulk of psychology classes were held, and the lab where the short-lived hotline had once existed. Campus was less crowded today, probably thanks to a heavy morning rain. The skies had cleared substantially, but Gwen suspected the showers had changed more than a few folks' overall plans for the day.

Lucas held the door at Garber Hall, and she hurried inside, pulling him along behind her.

They navigated the first floor to a set of closed office doors. Dr. Bloomsbury's door was the last on Gwen's left and standing open when they arrived.

"Come in," Dr. Bloomsbury said, spotting them immediately and stretching onto her feet behind her desk. She seemed to have aged by more than just six years. Her long salt-and-pepper hair was all white now and worn in a short bob around her cheeks instead of waves over her shoulders. She was thinner, too, and appeared more exhausted than Gwen recalled. Still, she had a ready smile as she pulled the tortoiseshell glasses from her nose. She let them fall against her chest, suspended by a delicate golden chain. Her gaze darted to their joined hands, then back to their faces. "Detective Winchester. Ms. Kind. It's lovely to see you both. Please take a seat." She waved a hand at the set of open chairs opposite her, then lowered onto her chair, as well.

Lucas released Gwen's hand and leaned forward in his seat, fixing Dr. Bloomsbury with his trademark cop stare. "Thank you for agreeing to see us. We have a few questions about the hotline project that took place approximately eight years ago. Do you recall it?"

Dr. Bloomsbury's gaze shifted curiously to Gwen. "Yes. It's where I met Ms. Kind."

"Gwen," Gwen interrupted with a cordial smile.

"Gwen," the older woman agreed. She turned her attention back to Lucas, then matched his no-nonsense expression with one of her own. "What's this about specifically? Your messages were brief and extremely vague."

Gwen cleared her throat and squared her shoulders. Then, she told her story.

Dr. Bloomsbury made appropriate expressions as the tale unfolded. She offered Gwen a box of tissues when she'd finished.

"I'm okay," Gwen assured her, "or I will be." She added a rundown of the last few days' events and how she suspected the hotline might've been where it all began, then waited for Dr. Bloomsbury's response.

The older woman sat back in her chair. "I see."

Lucas nodded approvingly at Gwen, and her insides fluttered.

Dr. Bloomsbury folded her hands on the desk between them. "Thank you for sharing your story with me. I'm sure it must be hard to go over it in detail like that. And given your timeline and experiences, I certainly understand why you'd come to me about this. But I don't have any information on the callers from the helpline. Those calls were all made anonymously."

"Maybe there's something else you can tell us then," Lucas suggested. "Anything will be more than we have to work with right now."

She raised and dropped her shoulders. "I don't even have details on the workers, thanks to the unexpected death of my laptop and a missing external memory device. I'd point you to Lewis, the grad student in charge back then, but he's out of town right now. Chicago, I believe. Designing social experiments with grant money earned from his continued work here at Bellemont. A very talented young man."

Gwen felt her knee begin to bob. "The student in charge of the hotline still works here?" she asked, wondering if maybe Lewis was the man who'd ruined her life.

"Several days a week," she said. "He's a teaching assistant, now pursuing his doctorate in psychology."

Gwen shot Lucas a look.

His chin dipped infinitesimally. "Did you say you have a missing thumb drive?" he asked, attention fixed on the woman in front of them.

"Yes, unfortunately. I lost a lot of work that week. I remember because I was writing my own research paper for publication at the time, and I lost both copies nearly simultaneously. When it rains it pours, I suppose."

Lucas patted the arms of his chair, expression thoughtful. "Maybe we aren't looking for a caller," he said. "Maybe we're looking for a volunteer, or Lewis."

Dr. Bloomsbury paled, but didn't speak.

Lucas turned to Gwen, an idea clearly taking shape in his mind. "What if her computer had help crashing, and the thumb drive had help disappearing, because a hotline volunteer, or its designer, knew his name and contact information would be on the drive, linking him to you?"

Gwen's bobbing knees froze briefly before taking

off again, hard enough to shake her chair. "When were your things stolen?" she asked Dr. Bloomsbury.

"Not long after the hotline ended. Before the end of the same semester, if memory serves."

"Before my first attack." Gwen kneaded her hands on her lap, trying to recall the names and faces of men she'd worked with at the hotline.

Lucas straightened. "Can you make a list of all the male hotline volunteers? First name, last name, nicknames. Whatever you can recall. And we'll need Lewis's contact information, as well."

The professor's gaze narrowed in concentration. "I'll do my best to recall the male volunteers, but it's been a long while."

"We understand," he assured. "Anything you can remember will be a great help. We can always contact the men you remember and ask them for additional names if you forget any."

"I think that's a guarantee," she said, pulling a pen from a mug on her desk and beginning a list on a sticky note. "I haven't thought of that hotline in years, but there were only about two dozen helpers and most were women, so the list of men is short." She scribbled words on paper, looking away for a few seconds from time to time.

A few minutes later, she passed a note to Lucas, then checked her watch. "These are the names I remember. I'm sorry it's not inclusive, and I hate to run off, but I have a class in a few minutes, and I need to set up my presentation before everyone arrives." She closed her laptop and loaded it into her bag while Gwen and Lucas rose from their chairs.

"Thank you for your time," Gwen said.

Lucas offered Dr. Bloomsbury his business card. "If you think of anything else, don't hesitate to call."

"Of course," she said, accepting the card, and trading him for one of her own. "Now you have mine, as well."

She turned to Gwen with an odd expression. "I hope you won't mind me saying this, but I'm proud of you."

"Me?" Gwen asked, wondering who the woman might actually be thinking of. Surely not Gwen, a college dropout and virtual recluse being openly stalked.

"Yes, you," Dr. Bloomsbury said with a grin. "You are a strong and dedicated young woman. You've endured the unthinkable, yet here you stand, searching for justice. Not everyone can do that. Bounce back after a personal tragedy. Those sorts of experiences usually have a way of defining us, but it seems you've decided to define yourself."

Gwen smiled. "I have. Thank you."

Dr. Bloomsbury nodded and took a step before turning back. "If I remember correctly, you were great on that hotline. Maybe someday, when you're ready and this is behind you, you'll consider working with others who've been through tough things like you. Maybe you can help them define themselves, as well."

She checked her watch again, then hurried away.

Gwen turned toward the exit, cheeks warm with pride.

Lucas slipped his hand over hers and gave her fingers a gentle squeeze. "I'm proud of you, too, you know."

She smacked her lips, feeling lighter than she had in a while. "Don't try to copy."

He laughed.

At the end of the hall, Lucas held the door for Gwen to exit and an arriving professor to enter.

The man stopped short of the door and placed a hand on his hip beneath his dress coat. "Lucas Winchester?"

Lucas released the door, shaking the man's hand instead.

Gwen took the sticky note from his free hand and reviewed the names while the men talked.

"Someone told me you became a cop," the older man said. "I couldn't believe it. You loved architecture so much."

"Still do," Lucas said, and the conversation moved quickly between them while Gwen examined the list.

The paper felt infinitely heavier than it was, and terrifyingly fragile in the growing winds. The small, thin sheet of paper with its minimal strokes of ink could contain the name of the man who nearly killed her twice. Nearly abducted her once. And had followed her for eight years.

A low ache formed in her stomach and rose high into her chest. The familiar sensation of someone unseen climbed the back of her neck like witch fingers. She turned to search for signs of an onlooker. She scanned the faces of people nearby, on the paths and on the lawns. None of them were looking her way.

She returned her attention to the paper, pressing a cold palm to the back of her neck. Stopping the prickles. She read each name slowly, then tried to picture their faces. Had she even met them all?

Then another face came to mind, and she tried to match his image to one of the names on her page, but couldn't. None of these names were his, but something told her his name was important.

Chapter Seventeen

Gwen waited impatiently for the men to part ways, then explained to Lucas about the other male student she remembered from the hotline. "We only met a couple of times. He was there for training, and I worked with him once. Otherwise I only saw him around campus, and not often. I assumed he dropped out."

"Can you remember his name?"

"No, but he was tall with dark hair and glasses. Definitely the loner type. He said he joined the hotline to meet people, just like I did." She took a moment to consider that. "Is it strange that lonely students were the ones who responded to the ad to answer calls at a loneliness hotline?" Presumably the kids who weren't lonely had better things to do, but still.

Lucas snorted. "I'll bet Lewis the grad student had a great time analyzing that."

Gwen frowned. "I hope we weren't the experiment."

"The callers could have been other grad students," Lucas suggested, further exploring the notion.

"That'd be awful. And deceitful."

"It would be disconcerting," Lucas agreed, "but

legal, depending on the wording of the contract participants signed. If you only agreed to take part in his project without specifics and qualifications, he could have done whatever he wanted within that context. It'd actually be better for us if the students answering calls were his subjects. At least then we'd have information on each of you."

That was true, Gwen supposed, but she couldn't help cringing over what she might've said on the questionnaire or during the interview. "Maybe we should contact Lewis in Chicago and ask him about it. He should have the name of the other guy I remember, too. If I describe him, it might jog his memory."

Lucas agreed, and they headed back inside. "I'll have my team run a background check on Lewis while we're at it."

She breathed easier. "Good."

After a full scan of the building, peeking in every door that wasn't locked, and finding a half dozen classes in session, but no signs of Dr. Bloomsbury, they admitted defeat.

Gwen's shoulders slumped as they moved back outside. "I guess when she said she had a class to get to, I assumed it would be inside Garber Hall. She could be presenting anywhere on campus. Or off campus for all we know."

"We'll call," Lucas said. "I'll leave a voice mail and send an email to follow up again. I live close enough to campus that we can get back here anytime she's available. Or honestly, if she can think of this guy's name, or wants to talk more about the hotline project, she can tell me by phone or email."

Gwen suppressed a sigh, disappointed to have to wait, yet again, before getting the information she wanted. She hated not knowing if something was a useful lead or just a random idea that went nowhere. "I could never be a detective. I have no patience, and everything feels so important. Not at all like things to be waited on."

"It's not for everyone," Lucas agreed. "Unlike food. Which is definitely for everyone. Hungry?"

She rolled her eyes. "Always."

"Good. Me, too." Lucas turned in the direction of the campus food court. "We never made it over to the student center last time we were here. Maybe we can do that now, and grab some lunch while we're there. Maybe a hot drink to keep us warm on the walk back to my truck."

"I like how you think, Detective Winchester." She smiled and offered him her hand.

He accepted.

They moved casually across campus, taking in the sights and sounds of homecoming week. Energy crackled in the air, despite the morning rain and reduced number of visitors. The Bellemont student body was unfazed. The school's spirit and pride were everywhere, from the banners and pendants to the occasional painted face and chest of a hooting male. Signs had been staked into the ground and erected at crossroads announcing the big game. Only two days away now.

Hopefully the nut terrorizing Gwen didn't have any

grand attack planned to commemorate the fifth anniversary of their first violent encounter. The unexpected thought tightened every muscle in her body and caused her steps to stutter.

"You okay?" Lucas asked, noticing instantly.

"Fine." They could talk more about the gruesome possibility later. Her newfound bravery was waning, and she hoped some food and caffeine would give her the pick-me-up she needed.

Lucas traced lazy circles against her hand with his thumb as they moved deeper into campus and her timelines became more entangled. Her traitorous body responded immediately, confused and elated. He'd always done that. Made the circles. And they'd always excited her. She'd imagined the gentle caresses as tiny messages shared by only them. A secret code for *she was his*. And *he was hers*.

She gave herself a mental shake. That was another time, and these circles meant nothing. They were habit, or muscle memory, at best. Something he did with every woman whose hand he held at worst.

She dared a glance in his direction and found him looking her way. Her cheeks flared, certain he could read her mind.

"It's strange being on campus together again like this, huh?" he asked, lifting their joined hands slightly and smiling.

Yep. Reading her mind as suspected. "I promised myself I'd never come back here. Now, this is my second trip in three days. I never expected to see you again, and I'm sleeping in your bed." The heat in her cheeks spread to her neck and chest. "You know what I mean. Everything about this week has been unexpected and weird."

He turned away with a single nod.

"But it's nice," she said. "Being with you again. Not the other stuff."

"You don't like my bed," he asked, a teasing glimmer in his eye.

She smiled. "You know what I mean. Your bed is fine." *A little empty without you in it but…* The train of thought brought her mind to a full halt. Did she want him in bed with her? For what?

A parade of images began immediately. Lying with him, beneath the covers. His warm hand stroking hair from her face, his gentle lips pressing kisses to her cheeks, nose and eyelids, whispering sweet promises into her ear as he left a trail of caresses from her earlobe to her collarbone.

She sucked in a breath, feeling her body come alert with the fantasy. It'd been years since she'd considered anything so intimate. She'd avoided the thoughts, afraid they would bring memories of the attack with them. But they hadn't. Now, on a campus she'd avoided, in broad daylight, a few tiny circles drawn on her hand had kickstarted her sex drive? Okay, maybe those long-dormant feelings weren't exactly a revving engine, but Lucas had definitely turned the key. She knew the fantasies couldn't lead anywhere. Imagining a man's touch and receiving it were two very different things. Besides, she had scars. Inside and out. Too many for even someone as wonderful as Lucas Winchester to overlook. And he shouldn't have to.

He pulled the student center door open for her, then followed her inside. "You've gotten very quiet."

"Just thinking," she admitted with a smile, unsure how they'd crossed campus so quickly.

He gave her a curious look, but didn't press the issue.

She longed to hug him for what he was doing to her. For the first time in too long, she was beginning to feel alive. Maybe her fantasies would never be anything more, but they were still major progress in her overall healing, and she appreciated the breakthrough Lucas had brought her more than he would ever know.

They ate bad chow mein from the food court and watched students through nostalgic eyes. Had she and Lucas really been that carefree not so long ago? She'd asked herself the same question on a regular basis since starting over in New Plymouth. Everything about her life there had always felt surreal. She'd assumed it was a side effect from her trauma, that she simply hadn't engaged with her world in emotional ways. Looking back, however, she wondered if perhaps the carefully created facade had never really fooled her. And maybe somewhere deep down she'd known it couldn't last. That she'd have to face the ugliness eventually, if she wanted to truly be happy.

And she did.

Lucas ordered two coffees from the cart outside the student center, then passed her a cup. The temperatures were falling, and it was a long way back across campus. They skipped holding hands in favor of cradling their steamy cups against their palms as they moved.

He nudged her with his elbow a few minutes later. "You really think it's been nice being with me again?"

She smiled against the rim of her cup, pleased she wasn't the only one thinking about them as they strolled. "I do. I'm glad I came, and I'm glad you became a detective. I don't know who else I would've trusted with my fear, and I can see now it was important I got help. I suppose it all worked out kind of perfectly." She hoped the man stalking her could see that, and that he blamed himself. He'd kept her isolated and afraid for a long while, but in the end, he'd brought her full circle. Back to the man she'd started out with, on the campus where they'd fallen in love.

A car alarm sounded in the distance, and Gwen jumped. She pressed a palm to her chest and laughed. "Sorry."

"At least you saved your coffee," he said, eyeballing the cup in her raised hand. He smiled, but it didn't reach his eyes.

She scanned the world around them. No one paid the alarm any attention, and eventually it stopped. Hopefully, she hadn't said too much and inadvertently pushed Lucas away.

He set a hand against the small of her back as they walked, and she wasn't sure why. Did he miss touching her now that they'd stopped holding hands? Did he want to feel more connected to her? Or did he just want to keep her close, like he'd said when suggesting they hold hands?

She wouldn't know unless she asked, and she wasn't ready to do that.

They sidestepped a group listening to a speech on global warming, then ducked carefully out of the way as crowd members attempted to snap photos of the speaker.

Lucas smiled over his shoulder as they passed. "You took more photos while we were dating than anyone I've ever known. Did you keep any of them?"

"A few." She turned away to hide her blush. She'd only kept a few if that parameter included hundreds.

His fingers bent and flexed against her back. "Me, too."

She dared a look at him. "You did?"

"All of them," he said. "I will find this guy," he added, changing the subject without warning. "The police forces in two towns are looking for him, watching and waiting for him to act out again. It's only a matter of time before he does, and he will be caught. That's a promise."

Gwen slowed, then stopped. She turned to him on the narrow cobblestone path between seas of green grass and bustling pedestrians. Then she took a step in his direction, and the noisy, windy, bonfire-scented world fell away. "I have never blamed you for what happened to me, Lucas Winchester. Not for a single second. Not then and not now. Do you hear me?"

He averted his eyes, casting his gaze over her head to scan the world around them.

"Hey." She poked a finger against his middle. "Look at me."

He glanced back at her before moving his gaze elsewhere.

She curled her fingers into the material of his jacket

and hauled him closer, careful not to spill her coffee or his. "You need to believe what I'm saying to you. I don't blame you," she repeated, fiercely. "And you need to stop blaming yourself."

His eyes snapped back to hers, mournful and full of regret. Emotion flickered over his face while he fought to maintain the careful blank expression.

"You said it wasn't my fault," she pushed. "Every time I woke up crying, convinced I was attacked because I knew better than to walk alone, even the short distance I was going, you told me it wasn't my fault. Now I'm telling you," she said, tugging again on his jacket. "It was never your fault, either."

LUCAS STARED INTO the most fierce and most loving eyes he'd ever known. "Okay," he answered softly, hoping he'd mean it one day. He couldn't imagine not blaming himself for what had happened to her and all she'd been through, but he could barely think of that now.

Right now, he was captivated. To say he'd missed her would be like saying he'd missed oxygen after being deprived of it for six years. Being with Gwen again was like unearthing the best parts of himself and realizing how much he'd truly missed them. He'd always known she'd taken a piece of him with her when she'd left, but he hadn't understood how much he'd needed them to feel whole. Standing with her now, in their tiny bubble made for two, her fingers curled into the material of his jacket, her warmth seeping into his long-dormant heart, he took his first real breath in years.

His free hand rose to carefully cup her narrow jaw.

Her eyes widened a moment, and he waited for her to step away or release him, but she leaned closer instead. The toes of their shoes already touching, she nuzzled her cheek against his palm.

Elation exploded inside him, and he ached to be closer still. He craved her kiss. To taste her sweetness, just once. He needed to know the heart-pummeling crush of emotion inside him wasn't one-sided. That some part of her had missed him, too. But he couldn't risk overstepping and accidentally pushing her away. Not now, when he still owed her the justice she deserved. He let his forehead fall to meet hers, wishing he knew how to help her heart find its way back to him.

His phone rang, breaking the spell and sending them each back a step.

Gwen looked bashfully away, setting her palm against her jaw, where his hand had been.

"Winchester," Lucas answered, hoping for good news.

"Hey, little brother," Derek said, his tone caught somewhere between mischief and regret.

Gwen slipped her hand into the crook of his arm, and they returned to walking. "What's up?"

"Oh, you know," he said. "Just swung by campus to check on you. Maybe give you a ride home."

Lucas frowned. "Give us a ride home?"

Gwen turned to look at him.

And the little lot where they'd left Lucas's truck came into view.

"Is that Derek?" Gwen asked, following Lucas's gaze into the distance.

Derek leaned against his Mustang, staring at a pile of broken glass, glinting on the pavement. Campus security guards held back a small crowd, and a uniformed officer snapped pictures of Lucas's truck.

"What happened?" he asked, towing Gwen forward, then breaking into a jog with her, as they neared the lot.

Derek greeted them, stuffing his phone back into his pocket and waving an open hand toward the mess, like a game show host.

Every one of Lucas's truck tires had been slashed. The side windows broken. And a brief but pointed message had been carved deep into the shiny black paint.

SHE IS MINE.

Chapter Eighteen

Lucas slid into the back seat of Derek's Mustang and moved to the center, hanging his arms over the edges of the seats in front of him.

Gwen took the passenger seat and shut the door. "Thanks for the ride, Derek."

He grinned, then cast a goofy look at Lucas. "I think your girl likes me."

"I've always liked you," she said, fastening her seat belt with a smile. She cast a regretful look through the window as they trundled past the tow truck hooking up his pickup for a trip to the body shop. "Sorry about your truck, Lucas."

Lucas grimaced. He was sorry about his truck, too, but more than that, he was infuriated to know he'd been followed again without knowing. Was he really so distracted with Gwen that he couldn't tell when he was being outright stalked? He was equally frustrated by the fact that there weren't any security cameras covering the small faculty lot where he'd parked, and that the son of a gun who'd ruined his paint job somehow believed that Gwen belonged to him. Like property. *Or a play thing,* he thought, recalling his own cat-and-mouse analogy. "Not your fault," he told Gwen, a little too late by the look on her face. "We know he's out there. It could be this beautiful Mustang next for all we know."

Derek frowned. "Watch it." He stroked her dashboard. "She'll hear you."

Gwen turned a bright smile on him. "You talk to your car?"

"Frequently," he answered. "I like to keep her happy, and you should, too. Since it sounds as if you're going to need a driver for a few days. Good thing I showed up when I did."

"Why did you show up?" Lucas asked, refusing to entertain the idea of Derek as his driver for a few days. "And how'd you know where we were?" Even if he'd heard somehow that they were on campus, it was a big place. How had he found the truck in a small faculty lot?

"I track your truck," Derek said, motoring into traffic outside the campus boundaries. "Your phone, too, but don't get cranky about it. I track everyone I love. You never know when someone might need help. Like now." He caught his eye in the rearview and smiled.

"You track my phone," Lucas repeated, misplaced anger boiling hotter in his chest. "What is wrong with you?"

"I care," Derek said. "I can't help it. I'm a caring guy."

Gwen laughed, and the sound drew both brothers' attention. She blushed in response. "I think what we want to know," she said to Derek, "is why you tracked us down. Did something happen? Do you have news?"

"Yes." Derek grinned. "I just got back from New Plymouth. I stopped by the design firm where you work and spoke with your coworkers."

"You questioned Gwen's coworkers?" Lucas asked, frustration mounting high and fast. "Should I even ask how you got them to talk to you? Because impersonating an officer is illegal. You know that, right?"

Derek made a get-serious face in the rearview mirror, then turned back to the road, splitting his attention between traffic and Gwen. "I told them the truth. I'm a friend of Gwen's from years ago, and I wanted to ask a few questions. Everyone was extremely helpful."

"I'll bet," Gwen moaned. "I've never told them anything about my past. They know my folks live in Florida and I live in town. I don't date and like to jog. That's about all I was ever willing to share."

"That would explain the intensity of their interest," he said. "They loved that we were friends from way back. They're all big fans of yours. I think your boss wants you to marry me," he admitted. "She's got a good eye. I'm not a bad catch."

Gwen laughed again, and Lucas joined her. Derek wasn't a bad catch for a woman not looking to catch anyone. Derek was too busy pushing everyone's boundaries and looking for his next adrenaline rush to settle down, and Lucas couldn't imagine a point in the future when that might change.

"Go on," Lucas urged. "Out with it. I swear you are the worst storyteller."

Derek's lips curved down at the corners, unhappy about being called the worst at anything, no doubt. "I learned that Gwen's coworker, Marina, stopped by her place to check on her last night. She said it was a last-minute decision. She'd debated all day because everyone knows Gwen's a private person, but she wanted to let her know the office staff is thinking of her and wants to help if she needs anything at all."

"Derek," Lucas warned, already at the end of his patience. "What happened when she stopped by?"

"That's what I came to tell you," he said, lifting a pointer finger into the air. "She saw a man on the property who said he was upgrading your security system. She thought that was a smart move given your situation, but she didn't get a name for him or the company."

Lucas's pulse picked up. Gwen's coworker had seen the stalker. Spoken to him.

"I didn't order any upgrades," Gwen said. "I already have their most comprehensive system."

Derek took the next right onto the expressway. "That's why I came to get you." He stomped the pedal and launched every horse under the hood into action, catching up with traffic in seconds. "I thought we could all go check it out together."

GWEN UNLOCKED THE front door, then stopped the wailing alarm. It plucked at her nerves to silence the system before the door was closed and locked behind her, but two giant Winchesters were currently wedged in the doorway, looking for signs of a previous forced entry.

"No one broke in," she said, leading them to her office. "My security camera sends alerts when someone opens a door or window."

She powered up the desktop computer and accessed her account with the security company. "The cameras also record when anyone comes onto the property. We can watch the feeds from here and finally get a look at this guy. If I'm really lucky, he looks right at a camera, and I can get a good headshot for police and local media. When did Marina say she came by?"

Derek shared the details, and Gwen brought up the day and time in question. Then they waited to see Marina's car slide against the curb. "There she is."

Lucas shifted over her shoulder, moving in close enough to smell his cologne and feel his warmth. "Did she say the guy was already here when she arrived?" he asked Derek. "I don't see any other vehicles parked along the street or in the driveway."

Gwen gave the scene another look. Lucas was right. There were vehicles parked in other homes' driveways, but none she didn't recognize, and definitely no commercial work vehicles. "He must come in a minute."

"Hopefully we can get a plate number when he arrives," Lucas said.

Derek hummed a little note of discord. "Actually, she said he was already here when she got here."

"Yeah, well no one's there," Lucas said.

Marina climbed out of her car, carrying a pair of shopping bags, presumably filled with wine and cake, then headed up the front walkway. She slowed before reaching the door, and looked to the left. "Hello?" she called. "Gwen? Is that you?"

Lucas pressed a palm to the desk, his body going

rigid. "She hears something. Come on," he whispered. "Come around here and show yourself."

Marina turned back to the door and finished her approach. She rang the bell then knocked. Undeterred by the lack of an answer, she repeated the process. When that didn't work, she skirted around the shrubs at the front window and pressed her face to the glass, using a hand as a shield for a better view.

"Wow," Gwen groaned. "She's really dedicated to this excursion."

"She seemed like the determined sort," Derek said.

Marina stumbled out of the flower beds a moment later, catching her coat on the bushes. She yanked it free, then marched around the side of the house, chin held high. "Oh, hello," she said.

Gwen and the Winchesters stilled, silently willing the man into the frame with their minds.

Marina returned a moment later, got in her car and drove away.

Derek straightened with a huff. "That was underwhelming."

"Did you at least get a description from her?" Gwen asked, feeling let down, yet again, by something that had seemed so promising.

"Yeah," Derek said, dryly. "He was tall. She guessed him at my height, then said he was around six foot two or three."

Gwen blinked. "You're only six foot."

"Exactly."

Ridiculous. Gwen's hope deflated completely with that hit. When it came to Gwen's nonexistent love life,

Marina remembered every minute detail, but when asked a simple, general question about a man's height, she had no idea what she was saying. "Figures."

Thinking of Marina and men in Gwen's life, something Derek said earlier came back to mind. "Did you happen to talk to an architect named Collin?"

He shook his head. "No. Just the handful of ladies in the front office and your boss."

Gwen chewed her lip, hoping Collin was still safe, and there wasn't a reason to worry.

Lucas shoved away from the desk. "We know this guy wasn't here to upgrade the security system, so let's figure out why he was here. We can start by making sure there aren't any signs of forced entry."

Derek moved toward the back of the house. "I'll check the patio doors."

Gwen went from window to window, checking locks while the men assessed the doors, then made a sweep of the perimeter. Everything was still locked up tight.

Unsure where to go next, Gwen made coffee while Lucas called Detective Anderson and brought her up to speed. Derek took a seat at the island and checked his email.

When Lucas made his way to the kitchen several minutes later, his expression was weary. "That woman hates me."

"Yeah," Gwen agreed, smiling over the rim of her mug.

Memories of the first time she'd met the female detective came to mind, bringing a new thought with them. She turned to Lucas. "Do you still have the email with the files from the copier?"

"Yes. Why?"

Gwen pursed her lips. "I'd like another look at those photos."

"What are you thinking?" Derek asked, setting his phone aside to watch her. "You've got that look. You used to look just like that before you took all my money in poker."

She laughed, surprised and pleased by the memory. "You let me win."

"Yeah, that's what happened."

"Here." Lucas handed her the phone. "What are you looking for?"

Gwen forwarded the email to herself, then hurried to her office. "Give me a minute."

The men followed her, impatient and eager.

She lowered into her teal, ergonomic chair, then accessed the file on her desktop computer. "I think we should look at all the photos taken at my place while we're here. Maybe we can use them to find his nest, just like we did at the hike-and-bike trail. Maybe comparing his two nests will give us a fresh lead."

"What kind of a nest?" Derek asked. "There's not too many places to hide around here."

"I don't know," she admitted. "Maybe a tree branch overlooking my yard or an empty home with a view into my bedroom." She could only hope the last suggestion wasn't a reality. "Lucas and I jogged the neighborhood a few days ago, but now that we have the photos, they can help us pinpoint where he stood to take the shots."

She brought up the images and began to sort them. It took several minutes to work through all the photos, moving pictures of her home or property into a separate file.

Lucas hovered while she worked. Derek watched from a few feet away, arms crossed and leaning against a yellow credenza.

"This is it," she said. "Now let's see what we can learn." She flipped through the images slowly, looking for consistency and anything else that seemed relevant. "The angles are all odd," she said, clicking faster, and shocked she hadn't noticed the peculiarity before. The photos all seemed to have been taken from somewhere near her home's perimeter, not somewhere distant and looking in.

Derek cursed. His arms dropped loosely at his sides and he moved nearer, watching as she flipped through the images on her computer screen. "Is he somehow gaining access to your security cameras? Stealing freeze-frames from your feed?"

"I don't think so," Gwen said. "My only cameras are at the front and rear door." She flipped to the feeds from the cameras to show them what she meant. Though, once she looked, she wasn't sure that at least some of the pictures couldn't have been taken that way.

Lucas headed for the door, and Derek followed.

Gwen worked to steady her breaths. Apprehension weighed heavily on her heart, anchoring her temporarily in place. If her stalker had access to her security cameras, then she'd never really had any protection against him at all. She'd trusted her system. Believed in her cameras. Believed she'd been safe inside her home.

She forced herself upright, then willed her feet to move. Just like that first time back on campus. One foot in front of the other until she was outside.

Derek stood on a large rock near the garage and shined a pocket-size flashlight at the soffit. "The walkway, mailbox and street sign were all visible in a photo of you getting the mail," he explained upon her approach. He extended an arm in a diagonal, pointing across the yard, creating an invisible line that intersected those three things. "The photo had to be taken from here." He climbed down, dissatisfied, then trailed his hands along the downspout. "But anyone standing here would've been seen."

Lucas stood in the mulch outside her front window and beside the door, running his fingers over and behind the camera. Muttering to himself as he worked.

"Ha!" Derek cried, turning her back in his direction. "Got it."

"Got what?" she asked, hurrying to his side. "What is that?"

"Camera," he said, raising a small, white item on his palm.

Gwen stared, a shiver of dread and realization coursing through her.

Lucas whistled, turning her around once more. He, too, held something on his palm. "He's not using your cameras. He's planted his own."

The men traded a look, then jumped into action, pocketing the uncovered devices and pressing their hands to her house. They traced every inch of soffit, spouting and white vinyl trim they could find, searching for additional camouflaged cameras on the perimeter. In the end there were two more. Hidden in plain sight, but blended seamlessly into their surroundings. Just like their owner in his ghillie suit.

So, it was true. He'd been watching her from her own house. Probably conveniently receiving the feed through his cell phone like she did. Being alerted to her and anyone else coming or going. He'd known the moment she'd arrived home or left and with whom. He'd known when she received packages and what food she liked to have delivered. He knew everything. And the blow hit harder than any fist, because it shattered her last notion of safety.

Even in the one place she was sure no one could reach her without invitation. He'd been watching. And he was probably watching right now.

Chapter Nineteen

Gwen thanked Derek for his help and hugged him good-bye. Being in his brotherly embrace felt just as safe this time as it had before, and she smiled as she waved. Ironically, she'd seen more personal healing in the days since the new reign of terror had begun than she had in years. No thanks to her stalker, but big thanks to her willingness to step away from her self-imposed quarantine and back into the lives of people who knew and cared for her. She suspected her coworkers would accept her, too, violent past and all, if she gave them the opportunity. It was the kind of epiphany she wished she'd had years ago, but was thankful to have had at all.

She powered her garage door up and smiled at her little sedan. Not a big tough pickup truck, and not a fancy sports car, but the simple base-model four door had never let her down. Derek's chauffeuring services weren't needed after all.

She grinned as Lucas folded himself into the passenger seat. His long legs bent sharply between his torso and the dashboard. "You can move the seat back," she suggested.

He patted around and pulled a lever, and the seat rolled back two inches.

She laughed.

"What is this? An airplane seat?" He tried again and managed a little more room, then adjusted the lumbar for comfort.

"You miss your truck already?" she guessed. "I'm sorry she was his latest casualty."

Lucas winced. "She's not a casualty. She just needs tires, a windshield and a paint job. That's like, new shoes and a makeover. She'll be just fine."

Gwen rolled her eyes at the analogy, then reversed out of her garage. She powered down the door. "I can't believe there was a camera right there and I never noticed it."

"I know," Lucas said. "Speaking of, I guess I'd better give Detective Anderson a call. We can drop these cameras off to her on our way out of town. If I had my truck I could've at least stored them in evidence bags."

"You don't think she'll like the freezer bags I had in the pantry?" Gwen teased. "They came with labels."

He shot her a flat expression as he worked the cell phone from his pocket, knees trapped against the dash. The phone rang in his hand. "That's weird," he said. "She's calling me."

"Perfect," Gwen said. "Maybe it's good news."

"It's never good news," he mumbled, then pressed the phone to his ear. "Winchester."

Gwen pulled onto her street then headed out of the neighborhood.

"I was just about to call you, Detective Anderson,"

he said. "We've got—" His words failed midsentence. "When?"

Gwen stopped at the next intersection and cast a curious look in Lucas's direction. Her heart pounded as the air thickened between them. Something else had happened. Something bad.

Lucas let his head drop forward, grunting occasionally as Gwen drove on.

Eventually, he disconnected the call and raised his head once more.

"What happened?" she asked. "Are we still going to the station, or should I go somewhere else?"

"We should probably head over to the county hospital," he said softly, pinching the bridge of his nose. "Anderson's there now. Collin Weinstein was attacked last night, and he hasn't woken up."

GWEN DRAGGED HERSELF into Lucas's house, after spending hours at the hospital waiting for Collin to open his eyes. He did, thankfully, but never for long, and because she wasn't family, she wasn't allowed to see him. According to Detective Anderson, and the details Gwen gleaned from the doctor providing updates to Collin's family, he was beaten in a way that mimicked her first run-in with the stalker, minus the rape. Detective Anderson suspected the similarities were meant to be a message to Gwen. Attacking Collin was direct retaliation for his perceived involvement with her, so the punishment had fit the crime.

She could only imagine what would happen to Lucas if the psychopath got ahold of him. She'd only had dinner with Collin. She'd been engaged to Lucas and was currently sleeping in his bed. Which she assumed her stalker knew, because he seemed to know everything.

It was after nine when Lucas pulled a bottle of wine from the refrigerator and looked at Gwen. "Do you still drink? And if not, do you mind if I do, because holy hell."

"Make mine a big pour," she said, sloughing off her coat and leaning heavily against the counter. "Wine has been one of my most cherished indulgences these last few years."

"Thank goodness." He poured two wineglasses nearly to the top, leaving only a small amount in the bottle. He tucked the bottle under his arm. "We'll take it with us so we don't have to come back. To the study?"

She turned without answering. She loved his study, and she was beginning to realize she still loved him. Wine would help her process that possibility, along with the three major disasters of the day. A vandalized truck. Discovery of surveillance cameras attached to her home. And poor Collin, who'd literally done nothing wrong, and his life was on the line anyway.

He hadn't spoken more than a few incoherent words before they left the hospital, but Gwen had faith for a full recovery. If she'd survived, Collin would, too, and she owed him everything when he did. His pain was on her. Like so many other things. Her silence about her past hadn't helped anyone.

Lucas flipped on the overhead light, then set the bottle on the coffee table. "When this place is done, I

plan to have a wine cellar. I've even thought of planting grapes and erecting an arbor out back."

"I like that idea." She took a generous sip and sank
onto the couch. "Wine is fascinating, delicious and it
unwinds me. Something I need right now."

"Agreed," he said, taking the seat beside her. "I prefer mine with some food, but I haven't had much time
to get to the grocery store lately. Feel like ordering in?"

Gwen tapped her glass to his. "Yes, and cheers."

Lucas took another sip of his wine before setting it
aside and breathing deeply. "I'm really sorry about what
happened to your friend." His expression turned tortured at the statement. "I was jealous of him when we
spoke by phone, and now I feel like an enormous jerk."

"You were jealous?" she asked. "Why?" The notion
didn't make any sense, and Lucas was always sensible.
More than that, he wasn't a jealous person. Two of her
favorite things about him.

"He's an architect. Young. Successful. And he's in
your life, a place you forced me out of." Lucas rubbed
his palms together, clearly ashamed and heartbroken.
"I wanted that life. Any life. With you."

Her heart gave a heavy thud at the possibility. Could
she still have a life with him? "Lucas," she started, her
mouth hanging open, then snapping shut, unsure what
to say in response. What were the right words to ex-
press complete joy?

He groaned. "You know what? Let's put a pin in
this and order that takeout." He grabbed his laptop
and opened it on his legs. "How about something from
O'Grady's? We can place the order online, then see

if we can find the Bellemont social media pages with photos from your freshman year. If memory serves, the school newspaper keeps dedicated web pages with highlights from every year. Maybe you were caught in some of them."

"'Bellemont Bests,'" Gwen said. "I forgot about those. I don't think I've ever looked at them."

"Me neither, but they came to mind while we were waiting at the hospital." He opened the O'Grady's website. "What sounds good for a very late dinner?"

"Something simple," she said. "Salad and breadsticks?"

"How about salads and potato skins?"

"Perfect."

Lucas ordered two of O'Grady's grilled chicken salads and a family pack of loaded potato skins. "Now, we've got thirty minutes to kill. Let's see what's on the 'Bellemont Bests' pages from your first two years."

Gwen braced herself, unsure she wanted to travel back in time when the present was complicated enough, and wishing they'd finished the conversation about a possible future with Lucas. She sipped her wine and focused on the screen as images from her freshman year appeared. All candid, and a few with captions. According to the *About* section, students were encouraged to send in their photos throughout the year for inclusion. Photos were vetted for appropriateness and added to the collection until finals, then the year was wrapped and it was a few weeks before the next year opened for photos. Meaning there were hundreds of pictures to wade through and very possibly for nothing.

Lucas ran his cursor over a small navigation menu and dropped a list down. "We can search by event or department of study. Maybe the psychology department commemorates its grad students' projects." He scrolled quickly to the right selection and clicked. A group of familiar faces stared back at her.

"That's us," she said, astounded. She marveled at the youthfulness of the faces in the photo, then jolted into action. "We need the list Dr. Bloomsbury made." She dug in her pockets, searching for the small page she'd nearly forgotten. "Got it."

She moved through the list of names on the page, comparing them to the list of names on the screen below a photo of the hotline staff taken on training day. She didn't remember sitting for a group photo, yet there she was, smiling brightly at the camera, with no idea what was to come.

"That's the guy I remember talking to," she said, tapping the screen with her fingertip. He was exactly as she remembered. Tall, lanky, dark-rimmed glasses. Bushy hair. She dragged her finger to the names listed beneath. "Scott Tracey."

Lucas looked at the screen, then at the scrap of paper the professor had given them. "He's not on Bloomsbury's list," Lucas said. "I'll ask her about him tomorrow."

Gwen smiled. "Good." She inhaled deeply, then sipped her wine. "Hey." She held the list up to the screen. "There's a name on this list that's not included under the photo. What do you suppose that means?"

Lucas compared the two, then retrieved his wine for

another sip. "Phillip Cranston." He frowned. "Where are you?" he asked the screen. He typed the name into the search engine under the year in question.

A photo of Phillip Cranston appeared in a group photo for the computer lab.

Gwen frowned. "He doesn't look familiar."

Lucas drew the laptop closer. "But he was part of the hotline and a volunteer in the computer lab, a place you frequented those years. I think it's worth digging into."

"Okay, and we still need to look more closely at Lewis, the grad student who organized this whole thing."

Lucas nodded, pulling his phone from his pocket.

She lifted her glass and smiled. "We make a good team."

"That we do."

She took a moment to enjoy the warmth spreading through her, courtesy of good wine and great company.

"I'll text my team and have someone run Lewis's, Scott's and Phillip's names. We should check their records, just in case." Lucas tapped the screen on his phone, getting the message out immediately.

Gwen sipped her wine and felt the knots of tension in her shoulders ease.

Lucas navigated to the "Bellemont Bests" page from her junior year. He stopped at a set of images from an impromptu party outside the auditorium where students had gathered after a concert. It was the night they'd met, and they were front and center for the photo. Smiling as if they already knew they'd soon be madly in love. "Look."

"I am," she said, marveling at the expressions on their faces. Complete happiness. "I remember that night." She'd thought of those moments repeatedly as she'd healed, physically, in the hospital. She loved Lucas so much, and she'd known it at first sight. "You made me feel so content," she said. "I'd felt sort of afloat until then. You anchored me. I shouldn't have taken it for granted."

Lucas curled his arm around her, bringing her closer on the small sofa and cuddling her against his side. "I will always be whatever you need," he vowed.

Gwen set her glass aside so that she could press a cheek to his chest and truly embrace him. She soaked in the peaceful vibes and let her heart accept how much she loved him. And the fact that she'd never really stopped.

Chapter Twenty

Lucas breathed deeply, inhaling the scent of her, and thanking his lucky stars that she was there. More than that, she was in his arms again and nothing had ever felt sweeter.

He tucked her tight against him with one arm, then set the laptop onto the coffee table with the other. Both hands free, Lucas cradled Gwen properly, protectively, and with both arms, the way he'd wanted to for so long. "I've missed you," he whispered, stroking her hair and holding tight to the moment.

"I've missed you, too," she said, her chest rising and falling with his.

"Should we watch a movie?" he suggested. "Something to take our minds off the night we've had? We can start fresh with new tragedies tomorrow."

She laughed, then groaned. "Definitely."

He forced his arms to release her so she could sit up, and he could choose a movie to stream. He decided on a small-town romance that she'd watched a hundred times while they were together. She'd jokingly called it her happy place when the stress of midterms or finals had grown too high.

He smiled as the movie began and recognition lit in her eyes.

She slid her arms back around him and squeezed, tucking her legs beneath her on the cushion and becoming a little ball of woman. "You remembered."

"Of course." He held her close as she nuzzled into him, and he let himself imagine that this could somehow last. That, maybe, ordering takeout and watching movies could be their new evening routine together.

She pushed away from him as the opening scene began, fixing a troubled expression on her pretty face. "I know this week has been an emotional train wreck, for me anyway," she added. Though she wasn't alone in that. "And I realize that all the bad things have served to enhance the good, but being here with you has felt a lot like being home. And that's a place I haven't been in a really long time."

She watched him with warmth and curiosity, taking in the surprise and pleasure on his face, no doubt. Then she set a palm on his chest, and let her gaze drop to his lips.

He covered her hand with his, and his heart beat against her palm.

Their gazes met, and desire seemed to break through her last remaining wall. She leaned closer, cautiously, then brushed her lips against his.

A fire lit in his core. The flames spread swiftly through him, urgent and needy. His hands ran up and down her back, savoring the feel of her as she took his mouth with hers. One kiss became two. Two became three. And with each fresh taste, Gwen's touch became less cautious and more fervent. More hungry.

She pulled back too soon, breathless and flushed.

Excitement danced across his skin at the sight of her like that. When she smiled, he let himself believe that she might stay when her monster was caught and her horror story was over.

He brushed the pad of his thumb across her lips, full and pink from his kisses. Already desperate to taste them again.

Gwen trailed her fingertips over his chest, then stroked her palm down the length of his arm, twining her fingers with his when they met. "I thought being near someone like this would be scary, so I've never let myself be close to anyone since you," she said. "Not after that night. And I told myself the reason was that I was broken by what happened to me. That I wouldn't be able to separate a man's intimate touch from memories of my attacker."

Lucas's heart broke. "Is that how you feel now?" he asked. "Are you…afraid?" He rubbed a hand across his mouth, hating himself for the possibility. Had he been adrift in pleasure while she'd been reliving her worst nightmare?

"No." Gwen shook her head and smiled. "Not at all." She pushed her fingers through his hair and traced the line of his jaw. "I can see now that I wasn't only avoiding other men because I was scared. Maybe at first," she conceded. "But I think the bigger reason is that I've only ever wanted you."

Lucas's lips parted in a smile. He nearly groaned in satisfaction. He'd never heard such perfect words. "Come here," he said, taking her hand and pulling her onto his lap. He stroked her crazy curls and stared at her perfect face, then brought his lips to hers once more.

Gwen took over easily, and he let her lead.

She sighed and moaned against his mouth as she shifted to straddle him, deepening their kisses and sending shock waves of desire through his body. Her warm, full breasts pressed against his chest. And her fingers ran over his shoulders, fisting in the hair at the back of his head.

He poured kisses over her neck and collarbone. She let her head fall back to grant him access.

Their lips met again, impassioned and easily parting. Tasting one another as their tongues moved sensually together.

He imagined rising to his feet with her, sweeping her legs around his waist as he gripped her perfect backside and carried her upstairs. But upstairs was too far. And it was too soon for that.

Gwen shifted her position once more, spreading her thighs wider and aligning their bodies so perfectly he could feel the heat of her through their jeans.

He broke the kiss to swear, and she laughed.

"Yeah," she breathed. "Me, too. We can stop if you want."

Was she offering him an out? Was she insane? Lucas grinned and shook his head. "No, thank you."

Gwen was protecting him, by providing him the choice she'd once been denied.

He wrapped her in a hug and rested his head against her shoulder. "I will never not want you. And I'll never stop craving your touch. I'd keep you with me forever if I could." The words were out before he'd thought them through, and he felt her tense in response.

She sat back, and he raised his head to apologize for ruining the moment. He swore again when he saw her tears.

"Gwen."

The doorbell rang, and she climbed quickly off him. "Food," she said, smiling politely and wiping tears with the backs of her hands.

He stood, shocked and confused at her response. His head still swimming from her kisses. "What's wrong? Was it something I said? Because the last thing I want to do is upset you or push you away."

She shook her head. "I'm okay. Happy, actually, and surprised. Did you mean that?" she asked, her voice small and cautious. "About me staying?"

The doorbell rang again.

Lucas growled. "Yes." He dug into his jeans for his wallet. "Very much. Why don't we talk about that over dinner?" When all the blood was back in his head, and he could make a solid case for her to stay.

She nodded, and he dashed to the door.

A man in the O'Grady's uniform stood outside, looking at the street, probably wondering if he had the wrong address.

Lucas felt his smile widen as he recalled the reason it had taken so long to answer the bell. "Sorry, man," he said, dragging the heavy wooden door open.

The delivery guy turned to him with a grin. "No problem." He handed over a box with hot potato skins and stacked a bag with chicken salads on top.

"Hang on," Lucas said, balancing the meal in one arm so he could pay the bill. "What do I owe you?"

"Everything," the man growled, pulling a Taser from his pocket.

The electrodes shot into Lucas's torso before he could drop the food or fight.

Fifty thousand volts coursed through him like a strike of lightning and his body went down with a thud.

Chapter Twenty-One

Gwen dried her hands on the small towel inside Lu-cas's first floor restroom. Her heart was light, and her mind full of hope as she smiled at her reflection in the mirror above the sink. He'd held her, kissed her and said he wanted her to stay with him. It was everything she'd hoped for, and they would soon discuss the de-tails over dinner. She checked her face and hair, then took a steadying breath as she stepped out into the hall.

The anticipation dancing across her skin became an instinctual shiver as she absorbed the gonging silence.

"Lucas?" She'd heard him open the front door and greet the delivery guy. Heard him ask how much he owed. So, where was he now?

"Lucas?" she called again, more quietly this time, as instinct clawed at her chest and neck.

She brought Derek's number up on her cell phone, thankful again for being back in her old world, with her old circle of friends. Friends who would fight for her, and friends who would forgive her if she called them in a paranoid snit for no good reason at all. Like, hope-fully, she was doing now.

"Lucas?" she tried a third time, peeking cautiously through each historic room.

Her call connected as she reached the foyer, and Lucas came into view. His limbs sprawled out on the polished wood floor, their meal overturned beside him.

"Hello?" Derek's voice broke through her panic, pulsing into her ear from the speaker on her phone. "Gwen?"

Lucas groaned and grimaced. He waved an out-stretched hand, trying and failing to form words.

"Lucas?" she whispered, shuffling closer, unable to identify the cause of his position or the reason he wasn't speaking.

He blinked pained, glossy eyes, and she knew.

Her stalker was in the house.

"Derek," she said softly. "Call 911. Lucas is hurt, and the stalker is here." Blood whooshed in her ears as she spun in a small circle, searching for the intruder. Could she hide? Should she run?

"Get out of the house," Derek demanded. "I'm calling this in on my work phone. You need to get to your car and go. Understand? Drive to the police station."

"Lucas," she whispered, a heavy round of shakes rattling through her body. "I don't know what's wrong with him."

"Leave him," Derek said. "He will never stop blaming himself if anything happens to you. Now, go."

She hesitated, hot tears falling fast across her cheeks. How could she leave him? What would her stalker do to him with unlimited time behind closed doors? "Derek," she pleaded. "Lucas would never leave me."

"Get. Out. Now," he demanded. He began to relay her situation and recite the address of Lucas's home. He must've made the call to 911. Thank goodness. Help was on the way.

"Gwen," Lucas slurred, his hand stretching in her direction. "Gwen."

She fell to her knees, prepared to clasp his hand, but he curled his fingers away, leaving only the pointer extended toward her.

"Run."

She heard the footfalls before she saw him. A tall, unfamiliar man stood behind her, a Taser in hand. "Phillip Cranston," she said, recognizing him from the photo they'd seen online. Phillip had been an assistant in the computer lab and a volunteer with the hotline. He was also the devil.

Lucas growled a series of animalistic sounds as he struggled to roll onto his side and get his legs beneath him. He made it onto his hands and knees.

Phillip swung his leg back, then kicked Lucas hard enough to make them both grunt. The force lifted Lucas's torso then flipped him onto his back once more.

Her blood ran cold at the sound of the impact. "Stop!" she screamed. "Please! Don't!"

Phillip pointed the Taser at Lucas, then pulled the trigger. Electrodes shot from the device, their metal hooks piercing Lucas's torso and sending his limbs into a frenzy. His back arched and his eyes rolled as Phillip held the trigger.

"Stop!" She lunged at the Taser, attempting to pull it from his grip. Ugly sobs raked up her throat as he moved it out of her reach. "You'll kill him!" she pleaded. "Please don't kill him!"

The worst of thoughts came then, towing a singular bright spot with it. This had always been the way her story would end, but it didn't have to be the way Lucas's ended, too.

"I'll come with you," she said. "Take me. Leave him. I'll do whatever you want. Whatever you say. Just please stop hurting him."

Phillip's wild eyes snapped to hers. He cocked his head like a puppy hearing a new word, then tossed the Taser onto Lucas's body. He grabbed Gwen's wrist and wrenched the phone from her grasp. It clattered to the floor with Lucas. Derek's small voice rose up to meet her as he yelled her name. "All right then," Phillip said calmly. "Let's go home."

He slid his fingers into her hair, knotted them into a fist at the base of her skull, then bashed her head against the heavy wooden door.

GWEN ROCKED AND swayed in the trunk of an old car. Everything smelled of rot and motor oil. Her head ached, and her stomach churned with every bump and jostle. Her hands were bound. Her mouth gagged. The latter had come after she'd woken up, realized what was happening and began to scream. She'd hoped someone would hear her and call the police. So, she'd screamed herself delirious from lack of oxygen and extreme inhalation of motor oil fumes. Then the car had stopped. Her lungs burned from effort. Her head felt as if it had been hit with a mallet. Her throat was on fire. The sweet night air had rushed over her when the trunk popped open. She'd gasped and panted, desperate for full clean breaths, but Phillip had calmly shoved a rag into her mouth, one that tasted like the trunk smelled, and he'd closed the lid without a word.

She fought continual waves of nausea as the rot and oil seeped into her tongue. She'd made her situation worse, and there hadn't been anyone around to help her. Only the stars and moon had seen, and she had no idea where they were.

She didn't know how long she'd been unconscious before she woke. Didn't know how far they'd traveled or in which direction. She'd thought they were on the highway, based on the speed they were moving, until the trunk had opened and there was nothing else in sight. Phillip's angry eyes had bored into her, setting off a flood of miserable memories. Even without the black balaclava to feature them, his eyes were unforgettable.

Phillip, however, had been completely forgotten. She squeezed her eyes tight and willed herself to find his face in a memory, any memory. Eventually, she did.

She hadn't met him in the computer lab or at the hotline. She'd met him in the library, her very first escape. He'd helped her get logged on to the online system for course information. He'd been the one to suggest the computer lab if she needed more help. They'd only spoken a short while, but she was sure that had been him. Except that Phillip had been kind and knowledgeable. Patient and shy. He'd told her he was from Kentucky, and he knew she wasn't. He'd said her lack of accent gave her away. But now, she couldn't help wondering if the first time she'd seen him was the first time he'd seen her.

The car turned and began rocking hard. The steady hum of tires on pavement had been replaced with the familiar crunch of tires on rocks. Gwen bounced and lurched inside the trunk, whacking her head against the carpeted floor until she was certain she would vomit or pass out from the pain. When she began to cry in misery and desperation, the vehicle jerked to a stop.

The engine went silent, and so did her world.

The trunk opened a moment later, and the stars were no longer visible.

Phillip had parked beneath some sort of makeshift carport. Instead of the night sky, there were old rotting boards and a rusty tin roof riddled with holes. He stared down at her, a vulnerable expression on his boyish face. "Sorry it took us so long to get here," he said, reaching slowly in her direction. "I had to be sure we weren't followed."

Gwen flinched, rolling deeper into the trunk, pulling away from his grasp.

He sighed, then grabbed her by her elbows and dragged her back to him. "You can't stay in the car all night. You'll get cold." He hefted her up and tossed her over his shoulder with some effort. As if she wasn't a grown woman, or even human. More like a sack of groceries or something to be hauled around. *Like a toy*, she thought. *A plaything under his control.*

Her head pounded with the sudden movement and slamming of the trunk. Her vision blurred and her stomach rolled until she was sure she'd be sick. She strained her muscles to minimize movement and combat the excruciating pain inside her head.

He crossed a wooden deck to some sort of outbuilding covered in limbs and leaves. Then he began the process of unfastening the padlocks.

She lifted her head slowly, turning it left, then right, searching for signs of life. Signs of people, homes or a road. Some way to signal she needed help. But there was none of that.

Silhouettes of trees were everywhere, backdropped by a deep velvet sky. The green eyes of night-things stared back at her from weeds and branches, watching as her life drew closer to its end.

HER ARMS SWAYED over her head, dangling past her ears, toward the ground. Her muscles ached from the clenching, a useless attempt to keep her still. She wanted to kick and fight, to get away and run, but she was useless like this, hurting and barely able to open her eyes.

He had her right where he wanted her, and they both knew it.

Inside the building, her world flipped and righted. Phillip flopped her off his shoulder and onto a couch that smelled of animals and dirt. She pressed her bound hands to her head, adding pressure to the pain and crying out when it only got worse.

Lights flashed on, blinding her and causing her to cry again. The wadded rag in her mouth stuck to her pasty tongue.

Phillip made a dismissive sound. He pulled the gag free and gave her a disappointed look. "You can scream all you want out here, but no one will hear you, and you'll just get yourself all worked up." He poked her bound hands with something hard and cool. "Here."

She pulled her hands back and squinted at the blurry water bottle in front of her.

"Take it," he said. "You need fluids to heal, and I bet that rag tasted terrible. You can wash that away."

"Where are we?" she croaked, her throat raw from screaming. She barely recognized her own voice.

He smiled, looking a bit apologetic. "Welcome home."

Gwen opened her mouth, and the extremely limited contents of her stomach poured out.

"You're going to have to clean that up," he said. "I'll let you wait until you're feeling better, but that's on you. Just like this place. I had a nice room set up for you at my house, but the cops are there now. Also thanks to you."

Gwen rolled onto her back on the couch, wiping sweat from her brow with the sleeve of her shirt. She forced her eyes open again and promptly wished she hadn't. The space around her was small and cramped, filthy and barely more than a shed. A card table in the corner held basic kitchen equipment. A coffee maker. A toaster. Canned foods and paper goods filled a clear-lidded container. Camouflaged gear and guns hung from pegs on the walls. And a collection of hunting knives was spread out on a toolbox beside his ghillie suit. "Hunting cabin?" she guessed, speaking more softly this time and hoping not to be sick again.

"Sometimes," he said. "This place is my secret, and it keeps my secrets. Unlike you." He pressed his hands to his hips, managing to look completely put out. "My dad always said you can't trust a woman. You're schemers, and a man's got to work hard to keep his woman in line or she'll step out on you."

"What are you talking about?" she snapped, the pain and anguish getting the best of her.

Rage flashed in Phillip's eyes. "I'm talking about how you were faithful for six years, and then you weren't. Now, I'm doing my part to fix that."

"I wasn't unfaithful," she argued.

He paced the small space between them in khaki pants and a polo shirt, as if he might be on his way to a nice office job instead of in the woods preparing to commit murder. Somewhere along their way, he'd removed the O'Grady's deliveryman shirt and hat. "Women always say that."

She moaned and closed her eyes against the pain.

"Drink," he said, pushing the bottle against her hands again. "You need to heal."

A new idea formed, and she opened her hands to accept the offer.

He uncapped the bottle with a satisfied smile. He wanted her to heal so they could live out his fantasy in the creepy shed.

She wanted to heal so she could get away.

"There. That's better." He helped her with the bottle, raising it gently, then wiping the dribble from her chin when she finished. "This would've been a lot easier if you hadn't talked to Dr. Bloomsbury," he said. "But you just kept pushing. Even after I'd warned you. And she gave you my name. Then you gave it to the police. Now I can't go home. And here we are."

"Cops are at your house?" she asked, a flame of new hope rising in her.

"Yep. They're at the office, too. Which is why I came for you early and how we ended up here. If I have to be stuck in the woods day and night, at least we can be together."

Gwen's stomach revolted against the water, and a round of dry heaves sent bullets of pain through her head.

Phillip dug his fingers into his hair and pulled. "I wanted this to be perfect. Bloomsbury ruined it. You can blame her if you want. I do. She's always had a big mouth. Nosy, too. She only remembered my name because she caught me watching you one day. During our loneliness hotline training." He scoffed at the memory. "She suggested I talk to you and reminded me that the whole point of being there was to make friends and to help others do the same. I walked out, and I couldn't go back after that." He offered her another sip of water.

She accepted, going easier this time to appease her stomach.

"No one besides Bloomsbury would've connected me to that program or to you. Not even you," he said.

He was right about that. "Why are you following me?" she asked. "Why did you start? What did I do?"

"Do?" He frowned. "Nothing. You were just pretty, and I liked taking your picture. It became a game to guess where you would be. When I was right, I rewarded myself with a photo. When I saw you struggling with your computer in the library, I helped you, and you were so appreciative. You thanked me again and again. I liked that. And I could tell you liked me, too. I thought about talking to you again, but I liked watching more than talking. And I already knew you liked me. It worked out for a while. I even turned the other cheek when you met Lucas Winchester. I liked watching the things you did together, and I knew you were thinking of me when you did them, so that was okay. I was thinking of you, too." He stroked a finger over her cheek.

She recoiled.

He smiled. "I lost my temper once, when you said you'd marry him, but you got the message. We fought, but you saw that I'm the one in charge, and you let him go."

"You raped me," Gwen said, pain and anger lancing through her. "You hurt me. I almost died because of you."

"I was angry. You made me angry. I had to do something or you were going to leave me. I only planned to talk to you that night, but you wouldn't listen."

"You didn't talk to me," Gwen yelled. "You haven't talked to me in eight years!"

"Liar!" He threw his hands wide with a snarl. His knuckles collided with a nudie poster on the wall, and it fell to the floor. Behind it were photos of Gwen and Phillip in romantic and even compromising positions. None of them were real. All of them were disturbing.

"What are those?" she asked, feeling the panic build in her once more.

He'd photoshopped their faces onto a number of erotic images and placed himself in pictures he'd taken of her life. "Us," he said.

Bile rose in her throat. And the truth of his words hit like a punch to the gut. "You think we've been dating for eight years? And that I didn't marry Lucas because you raped me and left me for dead on campus?"

He grimaced. His fists closed tight before him. "That wasn't rape. We were together."

"We weren't together. We've never been together. And I begged you to stop. I said no, and that was rape," she assured him, her voice ratcheting higher and louder with every word. A torrent of emotion ripped through her chest. "I begged," she repeated. "And you beat my head on a rock."

"We were in love!" he screamed. "We are in love. And women always say no."

"You're crazy," she said, feeling the crowded room grow impossibly smaller. "No always means no." The word slurred and her tongue began to thicken.

Her frantic thoughts became slippery, and her vision dimmed.

How many women had he raped? How many times had he justified the attacks to himself and to his victim using this sick mindset?

She blinked heavy lids at him, her gaze sliding to the bottle in his hand. "What's in that water?"

"Rohypnol," he said, moving in close and stroking her cheek. "Just a little something to help you relax. Drink this every day, and you'll be happy for the rest of your life." His fingers drifted lower as her eyes finally closed.

And she wondered how long that life would be.

Chapter Twenty-Two

Lucas fought the waves of electricity that had temporarily short-circuited his body, willing his brain and limbs to work together once more. He swiped the cell phone off the floor beside him, then forced himself upright. "Derek," he croaked, lurching upright. He staggered forward, falling against the doorjamb where traces of Gwen's blood still clung.

How had he let this happen?

"Lucas?" Derek asked. His voice boomed over the roaring engine in the background. "Where is Gwen?"

Lucas stumbled through the open doorway and onto the porch, letting the cold night air smack his face and bite his skin. The street outside was dark and silent. No traffic. No pedestrians. No Gwen. "Gone."

Emergency vehicles screamed through the neighborhood, their lights already flooding his street. Cruisers and ambulances typically arrived in ten minutes or less. Often, less. Which meant that wherever Phillip had taken her, they hadn't had time to get far.

"We need a make, model and plate on all vehicles

owned by Phillip Cranston," Lucas said, his training kicking in.

"Already on it," Derek said. "I called 911 right after she called me. I filled them in, then left. I stayed on the line in case she came back to it. I passed Phillip's name on to dispatch when she said it, but it sounded as if they were already working on him."

Lucas rolled that idea around, recalling slowly. "I sent a text to my team asking them to look into him before I ordered food from O'Grady's."

"I saw a cruiser at O'Grady's when I got off the highway. How much do you want to bet one of their deliverymen was robbed? Food, uniform and all?"

Two cruisers and an ambulance swung onto Lucas's block and cut the sirens. Derek's Mustang was only seconds behind.

Lucas bumbled back inside, careful not to touch anything he didn't have to as he grabbed his sidearm, jacket and badge. Then he reached for his keys and cursed. His truck was in the shop.

"Hey," Derek's voice boomed through the door behind him as a parade of medics and officers tramped inside. "What happened?"

The crew stopped, all awaiting the same answer. He recognized the lead officer as Brent Martin. One of the paramedics was Isaac.

Lucas swallowed his humiliation, stuffed his pride and emotions into a tightly sealed box, then relayed the events flatly. Just the facts.

Officer Martin looked up at the term *stun gun*. "You were tased?"

"Twice."

Isaac's jaw sank open. His hand was on Lucas's wrist in an instant, checking his pulse, before Martin had stopped speaking.

Lucas jerked free on instinct, but Derek's hands came down on his shoulders, holding him in place.

"Can you give me a physical description of the assailant?" Martin asked, fighting a smile as the Winchesters battled silently through a rudimentary exam.

"Yeah," Lucas said. "His name is Phillip Cranston."

"The man we're looking for," Martin said. "Good to know we're on the right track."

Lucas frowned. "We need to get out there and search the neighborhood. We might spot Phillip's car. He might've stopped for gas or supplies. Someone might've seen him traveling with an injured woman." His gaze jumped to the blood smear on his door.

"Be still," Isaac snapped, pressing a stethoscope to Lucas's chest. "You were tased twice tonight. Let me listen to your heart. Your guys are already going through the neighborhood."

"I want to go through the neighborhood," Lucas snapped back.

Isaac sighed. It wasn't a battle he'd win, and everyone in the room knew it. "Give me three minutes to finish evaluating you, then I'm coming along. My shift was up when I heard the call and recognized the address. I can go with you in Derek's car."

Defeated, and thankful for the support of his brothers, Lucas stopped fighting and let Isaac work.

Derek folded his arms and watched the police officers. He moved methodically through the room, gaze traveling slowly, sticking appropriately. To the cast-off stun gun. Dropped delivery food. Blood on the doorjamb. "He's good, but your girl won this one for you when she called me for help and gave me Phillip's name."

"We got the name from a professor," Lucas said, feeling the effects of the stun gun losing the last of their grip. "Then we found him online. I made the call to my team before we ordered the takeout."

"Blaze is at Phillip's place now," Officer Martin chimed in. "He went with the team to look for this guy after they ran his name through the database. Turns out Phillip Cranston has a lifelong record, if you count all the times he's listed on his dad's arrests for domestic violence. Textbook hot mess family situation in my opinion."

Lucas stilled. He knew what Martin meant, and a violent upbringing too often led to an out-of-control adult. Some kids grew up and broke the pattern, but too many were stuck in the rut. Those kids grew up repeating the mistakes of their parents, madder for it all the time, and lashing out harder as a result. Creating a vicious, dangerous, deadly cycle. "Tell me about Cranston."

"Dad was an angry drunk," Martin said, painting the ugly picture. "Beat the mom regularly till she ran off, then he beat a bunch of other ladies who came in and out of his life. Phillip stayed with his dad until college. He turned eighteen before graduation and had a number of arrests. Vandalism. Fighting. Domestic disputes. Things were quiet for a while after he enrolled at Bellemont. He moved onto campus, and his dad settled down when his overall health took a turn for the worse. He died a few months later, and it wasn't long after that Phillip's dates started filing reports with campus security."

"What kind of reports?" Lucas asked.

Martin's expression turned grim. "Stalking behavior and accusations of rape. That's why there's a team at his place and looking for him now. Even if he hadn't shown up here tonight, we had enough to believe he was Gwen's attacker."

Lucas felt the lid on his tightly boxed emotions begin to rattle. "He raped others before Gwen? And the precinct knew it? What the hell happened here?" Rage pounded against the waning calm.

"Reports were filed, but the investigations never led to any arrests. The women claimed to have been drugged. Their memories were unclear and inconsistent."

"Which is consistent with being drugged," Lucas growled.

Martin nodded again. "Phillip claimed to have dropped the women off after they had too much to drink. There were witnesses each time. He drove them home, then left. The rapes happened later that night. After Phillip was seen saying goodbye."

"He went back," Lucas said. "He planned ahead, set things up, then went back when there wouldn't be witnesses."

Martin released a defeated sigh, beginning to process the crime scene. "He could've unlocked a window or the back door while he was inside to pick them up for the date. Could've accessed their house key while gallantly taking them home, drugged. Lots of theories. No proof. As for the claims made about him following a woman his freshman year, they were in two of the same general studies courses. That put them in expected proximity on campus. Add in a communal student center, library and computer lab for all students, and two freshmen pursuing the same field of study are bound to run into one another frequently. She left Bellemont at the end of the semester."

Isaac stepped away, finished prodding and poking.

Derek spun his key ring around one finger. "Time to go. Officer Martin can lock up. I'll drive you and Isaac to meet Blaze at Phillip's place."

Lucas cast a look at Officer Martin.

He nodded. "Go on. We've got things under control here."

Lucas climbed out of Derek's Mustang twenty minutes later. Blaze's jeep and another unmarked precinct car were in the driveway. Every light in the house was on and the front door open. Neighbors watched blatantly from their windows and lawns.

The simple two-story home was in need of upkeep, and built in a neighborhood that had once belonged to the working class, but now belonged to landlords and the elderly.

Bruce, the senior detective on Lucas's team, met them at the door. He offered his hand to each brother. "Figured you'd be here soon. Blaze is already upstairs. He thinks he's running this show despite the fact that there hasn't been a murder or a single other reason for a homicide detective to be poking through our case." He craned his neck to shout the words up the steps behind him, then grinned. "All you Winchesters and your Boy Scout camaraderie."

Lucas clapped the older detective on his shoulder as he entered, thankful again for his family. Blood-related and otherwise.

Blaze appeared on the steps, headed their way. His expression was off. "There's something you should see," he said, skipping any measure of greeting and moving straight to the point. Something else Lucas was thankful for.

Lucas, Derek and Isaac followed Blaze through a first floor cluttered with officers and little else, to a back room lined with desks and monitors. The equipment was new and high-end, easily the most expensive things in the house. A tech officer was in position, scrolling through captured footage from outside Gwen's home.

Lucas's skin crawled at the sight of all the feeds. "So, this is where he watched her." When he couldn't be there in person.

Blaze crossed the room to a closet door and opened it. "There's more."

A collection of trinkets sat on a small table inside. A bracelet. A few hair ties. A handful of coins. Gel pens in pink and purple. Mismatched gloves and a pair of sunglasses. "We believe these are things Gwen has dropped, or he's flat-out stolen from her over the years," Blaze said. He tugged a string hanging over the items, and light erupted in the space. He pushed a line of hanging clothes aside. Behind them, the wall was papered in images of Gwen and Phillip in a number of false scenarios. "Looks like he used Photoshop to add himself into his surveillance shots of her alone and to impose their faces on the...other images."

Lucas moved closer, rage rattling that lockbox of emotions once more.

Phillip had pasted images of his face and Gwen's onto participants in a number of erotic encounters. She was never smiling. "He's demented. What kind of sick—"

"Freeze," Blaze said, cutting Lucas off and slapping his hand with an extra pair of blue gloves. "Don't touch anything without these."

Lucas's stomach pitched and rolled as he jammed his fingers into the gloves. He could only imagine what the psychopath was doing to her now, alone somewhere, knowing his time was nearly up.

Isaac moved into the space at his opposite side. "You okay?" he asked, hands hovering, ready to give medical advice or try to treat him somehow. But what ailed Lucas could only be treated one way. By putting Phillip Cranston behind bars for as long as possible and soon. "I'm okay," he told Isaac. "This guy's previous victims might not have had the evidence they needed to get him arrested, but I don't think there's a lawyer in existence who can get Phillip off now. Not when his creepy house speaks for him." He turned to Blaze, confused. "How'd you get a warrant to come in here like this?" The case had to be airtight, or Phillip would walk like so many others. "All I gave you was a name, and the officer at

my place made it sound as if Phillip didn't have any re-
lated arrests. Only allegations."

Blaze's gaze jumped to Derek, then away. "We used
photos taken inside the house to make our case."

Lucas tensed. "How'd you get inside his house without the warrant?"

Derek grinned his signature cocky grin. "I'm excellent at reconnaissance."

Blaze lifted a hand, stopping the conversation before it went too far. "Why don't we focus on finding
something that will lead us to Gwen? I've got one more
thing to show you."

"There's more?" Isaac asked, appalled. "I'm afraid
to ask what it is. At least it can't get any creepier," he
added more softly.

"Wrong," Blaze said, leading them through the
kitchen to a door with two padlocks, already removed.
He opened the door and flipped the light switch.

"The basement?" Lucas asked, a cold sweat breaking on his brow. Images from every awful case he'd
ever worked flooded his mind with dark and twisted
possibilities.

Blaze marched forward, leaving the obvious answer
to lend itself.

The trio followed dutifully.

Phillip's basement was typical. Unfinished, musty
and damp. Filled with old boxes and shelves of things
no one really cared about.

But there were bars over the glass block windows.
That part was not usual and definitely not good.

Blaze stopped at a doorway in a newly erected wall.

Dust from the installation still littered the ground. A line of padlocks hung open on the doorjamb.

Lucas stepped forward, drawn by morbid curiosity to whatever was on the other side of the wall. He pushed the door wide.

Thin vinyl flooring had been rolled out inside the space, covering the basement concrete. The walls were painted a serene and faded teal, like the accent color Gwen used inside her home. A small vanity and king-size bed had been placed against the walls. An armoire, rocking chair and two-seat dinette completed the furniture. The bed was dressed in white and piled high with lacy pillows. An old photo of Gwen and Lucas in a lovestruck embrace sat in a frame on the nightstand. Lucas's face had been replaced with Phillip's.

"There are cameras here, too," Blaze said. "They're monitored from upstairs, as well."

Lucas ghosted through the room, dumbfounded and sick. "He planned to keep her here? Indefinitely?" He'd never seen anything of this magnitude in real life. This was the kind of insanity saved for television dramas and horror movies.

Blaze rested a hand on the gun at his hip, his shoulders tense, expression blank. "Based on the amount of Rohypnol we found stashed inside an empty oatmeal box in the pantry, he planned to keep her drugged, and for a very long time."

"Detective?" A man's voice called down the basement steps.

"Yeah?" Blaze and Lucas answered in unison, then

caught each other's eye and headed in the man's direction. The others followed.

Blaze cut in front of Lucas at the stairs, then took them two at a time. "What do you have?"

The tech officer from the makeshift office gave the line of Winchesters a look, then turned his eyes back to Blaze. "You'd better see for yourself."

They tracked him back to the row of desks and monitors where a small cabin in the woods centered a screen. Infrared gave the feed an eerie green glow.

"It's another surveillance feed," the officer said. "I came across it while I was going through the files on the computer."

"Where is this cabin?" Lucas asked, certain this was the answer they'd been looking for.

"We're trying to find out," the officer answered. He lowered into the chair once more and took control of the computer. He backed the video up ten minutes, then pressed Play. Headlights flashed over the cabin, then went out.

"Was that a car?" Lucas asked. "Tell me we get a look at the plate."

The officer didn't answer. Didn't look his way. He just stared at the screen, drawing Lucas's attention back there, as well.

An image of Phillip appeared. He had Gwen over his shoulder like a caveman, her arms dangling limp and bound beside her motionless head. He worked the padlocks, opened the door then carried her inside.

Lucas stumbled back. Pressing his palms against

the cool surface of the wall to anchor himself. His head swam and the world tunneled.

Isaac clutched his arm and pulled him into an empty folding chair. "Breathe."

Lucas inhaled deep and slow, but there was only one thing on his mind.

Gwen's attacker had carried her, unconscious, into the woods, not to the creepy little room he'd made for her in his basement. He knew the cops were onto him. Knew he couldn't come home again. And that gave him no reason to keep Gwen alive.

Chapter Twenty-Three

Gwen opened her eyes to a blast of icy air.

Confusion became terror as the details of her night returned. Her pounding head and rolling stomach were the combination of a probable concussion and too much Rohypnol-laced water.

Her captor stretched a knit cap over his head, then stepped silently outside. He shut the door behind him, effectively cutting off the wind and delivering Gwen into comparative darkness.

Where was he going? And why?

She struggled to clear her vision and find a weapon she could use against him. She pushed into a seated position with a groan and a grimace, feeling a resurgence of pain in her still-healing side. Her still-bound wrists were sore and aching.

Through the filthy window, she could see the silhouette of him, standing frozen and staring into the distance. Down the path he'd driven the car in on last night.

She scanned the room again for a weapon she could manage and came up short.

His car keys, however, were laying peacefully on

the table beside his wallet and an unopened box of condoms.

Gwen's mouth opened and bile poured out, mixing with the contents of her stomach spilled there the night before. She wiped her eyes and mouth, biting back the tears. She couldn't fight like this. Couldn't run. And the things he would soon do to her were more than she could bear. He might not have assaulted her while she'd slept, but the ready box of condoms suggested it wouldn't be long now.

She steadied herself on the couch's edge, still struggling to gather her senses.

The white noise of a radio crackled nearby, and a voice barked out directions and coordinates. Orders and acronyms.

Outside the window, Phillip turned to face the cabin, anger painted across his face.

Gwen ducked. She surged forward, scraping the keys off the table, then diving back onto the nasty couch. A plume of dirt and animal hair rose around her as she pushed the keys between the cushions and closed her eyes. Her nose itched and eyes burned, but she couldn't gag, couldn't whimper or sneeze. Couldn't let him know she was awake. If he knew that, he'd also know she was the one who'd taken the keys.

The door swept open, filling the small space with another gust of icy air, and Phillip stormed inside. He slammed the door behind him, and her shoulders jumped involuntarily. He went to the table, listening intently to the rambling voice Gwen now recognized as a police dispatcher, delivering details of local law enforcement's hunt for him.

Phillip removed his phone from his pocket, then powered it down with a curse. He pulled the battery and SIM card, then threw the phone against the wall.

Gwen jumped again without intention, and her assailant looked her way. "Where am I?" she asked, not needing to fake the grogginess in her tone or expression. "What happened?"

He scowled. "They're coming. So, we're going. I'll take my car as far as I can, then swap it for something else." He looked her over, contemplating. "You look awful. I can't take you in public like that." He reached for her, roughly pulling her into a seated position. He tried to smooth her wild curls, then stuffed a ball cap over them instead.

She whimpered as the material scraped against her cut and aching forehead.

"Put this on," he said, grabbing a jacket from a hook near the door and tossing it in her lap.

"My hands," she said, raising her bound wrists and blinking to clear her vision.

Phillip cursed. His gaze swept over her, then around the cabin, presumably in search of a plan.

Gwen's plan was to stall. If she understood the situation correctly, help was closing in, and Phillip didn't plan to kill her and dispose of the evidence. He planned to take her with him. She could work with that. "I need to lie down," she said, swooning backward, pretending to go boneless from the drugs.

His expression lit. "That's perfect." He grabbed the water bottle from the table and forced it against her mouth. "Drink."

Her gut knotted at the idea of going under again. She let her eyes drift shut. She couldn't drink that water.

"If you drink this, I won't put you in the trunk again," he said. "You can sleep up front with me. I'll even remove your zip ties." He tapped a finger to the plastic bindings.

Untied and not in the trunk were two things she needed to be if she was going to escape.

She nodded slowly, then let him put the bottle to her lips. She sipped gingerly, making more noise than necessary and holding the small amount in her mouth.

He watched her swallow, then breathed a sigh of relief. "I'll get the knife for this," he said, touching the binding again.

When he turned away, Gwen buried her face in the disgusting cushion where her head lay and spilled the water from her mouth into the fabric. She pressed her cheek and hair against the wet spot before he turned back, wishing she hadn't swallowed any, but thankful for the amount she was able to reserve and spit out.

Phillip cut the ties with a pocketknife he pulled from a coat pocket, and she let her hands fall limply to her sides. "Okay," he said. "We have to go, and you need to keep drinking to stay hydrated." He set the bottle beside her, then pulled her up again. "Let's get your coat on and get out of here."

He fed her arms into the oversized sleeves of a black men's coat, then pulled her onto her feet.

She fell against him, overacting possibly, but he didn't seem to notice. His distraction grew with every new syllable from the police scanner in the corner.

"Where are my keys?" He patted his pockets and turned in a small circle, dragging her with him. "I put them on the table," he said.

Gwen bent her knees, sliding down his body and forcing him to set her back on the couch.

He crouched onto the floor, searching desperately for his missing keys.

Gwen slipped a hand up to the water bottle and loosened the cap until it spilled over the cushions near her face. She coughed and choked, as if she'd been trying to drink.

"Hey!" Phillip glared in her direction, clearly seeing the nearly empty bottle and furious about it. "What did you do? That's all the water I had for you. Now it's gone!"

She forced her expression to remain slack and her body still, but internally, she wanted to run. Adrenaline pumped hard in her veins, preparing her to take action, whatever that might be.

"Radio silence," the dispatcher called. "In three, two…" And the voice was gone. Only white noise remained.

Phillip jolted upright with a wail and a curse. He punched the wall in a rage, then slammed his fists on the table before kicking everything in sight, including the couch where Gwen lay. He whacked the water bottle off the cushion near her cheek, then spun suddenly away.

She pressed her eyelids shut, terrified he would rip one of the guns from the wall and kill them both rather than be caught or surrender.

The rustle of fabric pulled her eyes open a moment later, though her lids felt heavier than before.

Phillip had stepped into his ghillie suit and pulled on the balaclava. "They can't have you," he said coolly. "I won't allow it." He yanked a rifle with a scope off the rack near the door, and he walked outside.

Lucas secured the straps of his bulletproof vest and tucked a small communications device into his ear while members of the Jefferson County Sheriff's strike team made battle plans.

It was a bit of a shot in the dark, but the plot of tax-delinquent property in the middle of nowhere was the only hope Lucas had. Public records showed the property had belonged to Phillip's father and had been inherited by Phillip upon his father's death. There were no known structures or road frontage, but it was remote and familiar to Phillip. The perfect place for a psychopath under pressure to rest and regroup.

Lucas zipped his coat, tugged on his hat, then freed his sidearm from its holster. He nodded at the strike team captain who'd taken Lucas's call, and he'd mobilized a squad while Derek had raced Lucas across the county to join them.

Now, they moved in single file, up a rutted, leaf-covered lane into the wilderness, while the first fingers of dawn climbed the trees.

GWEN GRIPPED THE WINDOWSILL, steadying her body and wishing she hadn't swallowed any of the drugged water, but feeling the impact of the amount she had.

Phillip moved like a ghost through the trees beyond the window, looking completely at ease. As if he'd done the same thing a hundred times, *which he had*, she realized, while stalking her. He squatted in a thicket twenty-five yards away, then set the barrel of his gun in the deep V of a dying tree and pointed it down the muddy pitted path they'd taken to the cabin.

Gwen counted to ten, making sure he was staying put. Then she reached for the radio and turned up the volume. She needed the dispatcher's voice to come back. Needed to know what was happening out there, and needed to warn whoever was coming that Phillip was lying in wait.

She considered digging the car keys from the couch and attempting to drive away, but how far could she really get? Without being shot? Falling down? Or hitting a tree? The cabin slanted beneath her feet, as if confirming her inability to get far on her own. She stumbled toward the couch, woozy again and desperate to sit before she fell. Her toe connected with something small and hard on the way.

Phillip's cell phone skated across the floor, and Gwen nearly cried in response.

She dropped to the floor, chasing the device beneath the table and begging her eyes to stay open. She found the battery near the wall, then rushed to install it before Phillip shot someone or came back for her.

Adrenaline and panic made her clumsy. She dropped the battery twice before getting it into place. And she powered up the device, praying for a signal.

That was when she heard the first gunshot.

THE BARK ON the tree beside Lucas's head burst into shreds, sending him skidding onto his knees behind it. His ears rang and his heart raced. He wasn't sure if that had been a warning shot, or if Phillip had missed. Neither seemed possible.

"Winchester?" The voice of the strike team captain sounded in his ear.

Lucas touched the communications device with one fingertip. "I'm okay," he said. "I wasn't hit."

"Did you see where the shot came from?" he asked.

"East," he huffed, trying desperately to slow his sprinting heart. "That's all I've got."

And it wasn't good news. At this time of day, a position in the east put Phillip between the lawmen and the sun. Phillip would have a clear view of them as day broke, and they would have a blinding view of the rising sun.

Still, a slow smile spread over Lucas's face as he pressed his back to the tree. The gunshot meant they'd found Phillip. And if they'd found Phillip, they'd also found Gwen.

GWEN WATCHED PHILLIP through the cabin window, nearly invisible in the trees. Her heart pounded harder

than her head at the sound of the gunshot. "He's shooting," she told the emergency dispatcher on the other end
of the line. "I think he just shot at someone." She hated
herself for hoping it wasn't Lucas. Or Blaze. She knew
neither of those lawmen would stay away from a rescue
mission meant to save her. And she was sure Derek and
Isaac would be there, too, if they could. Gwen's parents
might live in Florida, but she had plenty of family, she
realized, right here in Kentucky, and she loved them all.

So, she wouldn't let this psychopath sit out there and
pick them off one by one.

"Can you communicate with whoever's here for me?"
she asked the dispatcher. "Tell them I'm here in the
cabin, and I'm okay. Tell them Phillip's in his ghillie
suit and that he took a rifle with him. He's using a tree
as cover and a gun rest. I can see him from here. Maybe
twenty-five yards from the cabin. I'd run, but I don't
think I can, and I'm sure he'll see me open the door."

"What if we can give you some cover?" a male voice
asked in her ear.

"What?" she gasped, unsure what had happened to
the female dispatcher's calming voice, or who she was
hearing now.

"Ms. Kind," the dispatcher said. "I've got Jerry Hor-
ton, on the line. He's our strike team captain, and he's
got men in place to bring you home."

Tears welled and fell from Gwen's eyes. Her chest
heaved with a grateful sob, and the knot in her chest
constricted impossibly tighter. She wasn't sure she
could actually run, but she would make a break from

the cabin if this man told her to. "I'll try," she croaked, "but I've been drugged."

There was a long beat of silence before Jerry spoke again. "Hold the line," he said finally.

Panic swept through her at the silence. What did that mean? Had he changed his mind? Had something bad happened outside? Why hadn't she asked about the gunshot?

"Ms. Kind?" the dispatcher said once more. "I won't leave you. Hang in there while he makes arrangements. Can you still see the shooter?"

Gwen jerked her gaze back through the window, terrified he'd moved while she'd been distracted. "I don't know." She stared hard into the woods, willing Phillip to move, if he was there. Just enough for her to confirm. "The shot," she said, her voice shaky with fear. "Did he hurt anyone?"

"No, ma'am."

A fresh punch of tears blurred Gwen's vision, and she blinked them away. "Good."

A moment later, wind rustled through the forest fluttering the material of Phillip's suit, and she nearly collapsed with relief. "I see him," she said. "He hasn't moved."

"Excellent work," the dispatcher praised. "Now, we'll stand by and wait for orders. You doing okay?"

"No," she whispered, her limbs beginning to shake severely. "I don't think I can do this."

"Ms. Kind," the woman on the other end of the line responded, patiently. "I'm sure you feel that way right now, but from what I hear, you can do anything. I've been told you're a fighter, a survivor and the reason those men are out there. Reports coming through our office this morning say you called someone when you suspected an intruder, and you gave Phillip Cranston's name to the police before he took you. You've been stabbed, choked and probably concussed. You're currently drugged, yet you found a way to call me. And it's because of you we now know the gunman's position. So, whatever Jerry wants you to do, I am certain enough for the both of us that you can and will get it done."

Gwen's knees buckled, and she cried. She didn't hold back. Didn't have the strength left to fight the tidal wave of emotions. And more than anything, she just wanted to lie down and close her eyes. Just for a minute.

"Ms. Kind?" Jerry's voice boomed again in her ear. "We're ready for you. I'm going to count to three, then instruct my men to open fire in the direction of the shooter. Twenty-five yards to the east of the cabin. Right?"

She pulled her eyelids open, unsure when they'd shut. "Yes," she whispered, her limbs going slowly numb from the drugs.

"When you hear the first shots fired, you're going to open that cabin door, and you're going to run. One foot in front of the other. Northwest. That's behind the cabin and away from the shooter. We'll do the rest. Don't stop running until you reach us. We're moving into position for your recovery now."

The line went quiet.

"Phillip Cranston." The strike team captain's voice echoed strong and loud through the world outside, possibly through a bullhorn. "This is the Jefferson County Sheriff's department, and you're under arrest for the kidnapping of Gwen Kind. Lay your weapon down, and come out where I can see you, or we'll be forced to open fire."

Another shot rang out, and Gwen knew that was Phillip's response. He wouldn't give up or surrender, and someone was likely to die today.

It couldn't be her.

She pushed onto her feet once more and reached for the cabin door.

The forest exploded in a hail of gunfire.

And she ran.

Gwen's feet pounded loud and awkward against the wooden planks outside the cabin, shaking the platform beneath her. She gripped the wall at the corner as she leapt into the forest and bumbled quickly away, leaving the cabin door agape behind her.

Her legs were weak and noodle-y, her breaths coming loud and fast. And her head split with the continuous sound of gunfire.

Still, she stumbled forward, gripping trees for support, then pushing off them for momentum. *One foot in front of the other*, she told herself. And then she saw him.

A blurry silhouette in black raced confidently through the trees before her, his presence instantly familiar and more comforting than anything she'd ever known. Her guardian angel, her personal protector, the only man she'd ever love. Lucas Winchester.

Epilogue

Gwen hurried to answer the door at Lucas's home for the fifth time in an hour. His brothers, parents and half the local police force were already gathered in the kitchen, laughing, chatting and generously splattered in paint. The party had been Lucas's idea. The painting part was Gwen's, though she'd yet to pick up a brush. "I've got it," she called, padding back across the layered sheets of plastic protecting restored hardwood floors.

It had been two months since her personal testimony, along with Lucas's professional one, had helped put her abductor, rapist and stalker away for twenty-six years. When something went that right in life, she had to agree, it was cause for celebration. So, she'd ordered eighty gallons of carefully selected custom paints, enough local takeout to feed an army and invited all their friends.

As for Phillip's testimony, it had been an unfortunate one. He was raised in a dark, twisted place by a dark, twisted man, and while Phillip had gotten some distance by moving out for college, the serious long-term damage had already been done. And it deeply tainted his every encounter with the women on campus. He wanted them to want him, but he also wanted to hurt them. And his frustrations became obsessions. Gwen had simply been in the wrong place at the wrong time when she asked for help in the library. When she'd taken his advice and visited the computer lab the next day, he'd seen it as their first date.

He'd testified that he regretted hurting her so badly back then. He didn't, however, regret that he'd done it, because for six years afterward, things had gone well in his mind. She'd broken the engagement like he'd wanted, and she'd stopped seeing anyone but him.

Gwen shook her head at the memory. Even on the stand, Phillip didn't fully accept that his relationship with her was totally in his mind. Or that hurting people wasn't the way to show them he cared.

She smiled at the sounds of laughter echoing through her home, then pulled herself back to the moment and opened the door.

"Surprise!" a chorus of female voices called.

Her coworkers stood on the doorstep, each with flowers or a bottle of wine. "Housewarming gifts," Marina said, passing a bottle of merlot from her hands to Gwen's.

Her boss, Victoria Noble, shot a knowing look at her, then handed over a bouquet of flowers. "I'm not here to paint, but you know I can't miss an opportunity to tour a home like this one."

"Come in!" Gwen said, pulling them all inside. Victoria had told Gwen not to hurry back to work after her abduction, but Gwen had been back in her place as quickly as possible. Eager to get it over with. Answer all the uncomfortable questions, field the rampant gossip and adjust to the pitying looks. Instead, her coworkers had been impressively understanding. No gossip. No pity. Just lots of warm hugs and a "Welcome Back" cake. "I'm glad you could all come."

"We wouldn't miss it," Victoria said, admiring the history all around her. "This home is stunning."

"Thank you," Gwen said, feeling immediately proud. She and Lucas had made a thousand plans for the home over late-night glasses of wine and old movies they barely watched. She wanted to pinch herself every time she thought of how lucky she was to be here with him now.

Except, he wasn't there now. She checked the grandfather clock in the corner and frowned. Lucas had gone to run an errand more than an hour ago, and logical or not, she was beginning to worry.

Marina and Debbie hurried toward the kitchen, eager to join in on the chatter and laughter.

Victoria followed more slowly, her eye for design and love of history giving her pause at every glorious detail. "The two of you talked about living in this home together some day, back when you were in college?"

Gwen nodded, biting her lip and feeling impossibly blessed. "Yep. And even after all that had happened to me, to us," she corrected, "he bought the place as planned and began the renovations himself."

"Now, here you are together, as planned," she echoed Gwen's words. "Romantic." Victoria dragged a fingertip over the intricately detailed woodwork along the staircase. "And absolutely stunning."

Gwen's smile eased as something else came to mind. "Have you heard from Collin?" She posed the question every day and usually received the same response. He was recovering nicely, but not feeling like visitors. She couldn't help blaming herself for what he'd been through, and she knew firsthand what he might be feeling.

"I did," Victoria said, turning on her toes with a grin. "Collin called around dinner last night and caught me at the office. It seems he's fallen head over heels for his physical therapist and has officially resigned from his position at my company." She arched her brows. "He's moving to the therapist's town, about ninety minutes away, and he asked me for a letter of recommendation. I agreed, of course, but oh, to be young again," she mused.

Gwen laughed, and the doorbell rang. "I'll be right back," she said with a small sigh, eager to spend more than a few minutes with each guest and dying to actually paint something.

The music quieted behind her as she opened the door once more, hoping it would be Lucas and knowing he wouldn't have rung the bell.

She froze at the sight of two people she hadn't seen since the trial, then smiled immediately in response to their bright faces. "Mom? Dad?"

They engulfed her in a hug, pulling her into the house with them and closing the door.

"We missed you, sweet baby girl," her mother cried.

"I missed you, too." Gwen squeezed them tighter before letting go. She wished she could keep them with her forever. "What are you guys doing here? Is everything okay in Florida?"

Her dad stepped back with a huff. "Everything's hot in Florida. Lucas picked us up from the airport."

Gwen smiled. "So, that was where he went."

"He'll be right in," her mom assured her. "We were thrilled to get his call and invitation."

"Lucas invited you to our painting party?"

Her mom laughed and slid in close to her husband's side. "Not exactly. Lucas wanted to talk to us in person."

"About what?" she asked, mystified.

"About asking you to marry me," Lucas said, his voice breaking the sudden silence all around her.

Gwen spun to find him and all their previously chatty guests in a loose crowd behind her, silent and grinning from ear to ear.

Lucas lowered onto one knee, and the air left her lungs.

He started by telling her he loved her, and she picked up other words here and there. *Teammates. Soulmates. Lovers. Friends.* But louder than all his sentiments and promises was the look in his eye and the answering response of her heart.

She accepted the ring he presented with a kiss and plenty of tears. Because it wasn't just any ring. It was her ring. The one he'd given her six years ago. The one they'd found together at an estate sale. Probably as old, and definitely as beautiful, as their home. And she promised again that she would cherish it forever. The same way she cherished him, for all of the days of her life.

* * * * *

Look for the next book in Julie Anne Lindsey's Heartland Heroes miniseries,
Protecting His Witness,
available next month wherever Harlequin Intrigue books are sold!

SPECIAL EXCERPT FROM

⊞ HARLEQUIN

INTRIGUE

*LAPD detective Jake McAllister has his work cut out
for him trying to identify and capture a serial killer
hunting women. The last thing he needs is victims' rights
advocate Kyra Chase included on his task force. He
senses trouble whenever she's around, and not just to
his hardened heart. It also seems she might have a very
personal connection to this most challenging of cases…*

*Keep reading for a sneak peek at
The Setup,
the first book in A Kyra and Jake Investigation,
from Carol Ericson.*

He'd recognize that voice anywhere, even though he'd
heard it live and in person just a few times and never
so…forceful. He believed her, but he had no intention
of letting her off the hook so easily.

He raised his hands. "I'm LAPD Detective
Jake McAllister. Are you all right?"

A sudden gust of wind carried her sigh down the trail
toward him.

"It…it's Kyra Chase. I'm sorry. I'm putting away my
weapon."

Lowering his hands, he said, "Is it okay for me to
move now?"

"Of course. I didn't realize… I thought you were…"

"The killer coming back to his dump site?" He flicked on the flashlight in his hand and continued down the trail, his shoes scuffing over dirt and pebbles. "He wouldn't do that—at least not so soon after the kill."

When he got within two feet of her, he skimmed the beam over her body, her dark clothing swallowing up the light until it reached her blond hair. "I didn't mean to scare you, but what are you doing here?"

"Probably the same thing you are." She hung on to the strap of her purse, her hand inches from the gun pocket.

"I'm the lead detective on the case, and I'm doing some follow-up investigation."

"Believe it or not, Detective, I have my own prep work that I like to do before meeting a victim's family. I want to have as much information as possible when talking to them. I'm sure you can understand that."

"Sure, I can. And call me Jake."

Don't miss
The Setup *by Carol Ericson,*
available April 2021 wherever
Harlequin Intrigue books and ebooks are sold.

Harlequin.com